A Love Awakened

Or

The Cross Roads in Life

By G. H. Teed

Illustrated by J. R. Burgess

First published in the Answers' Library magazine,
No. 371, 30 June 1917.

Stillwoods Edition

Stillwoods.Blogspot.Ca

Catalogue Information:
Title: A Love Awakened
Subtitle: The Cross Roads in Life
Author: G. H. Teed (1881-1938)
Illustrated by: J. R. Burgess
First published anonymously in the Answers' Library magazine, No. 371, 30 June 1917.
This Edition by: Stillwoods, 2022
ISBN Canada: 978-1-989788-94-3
Blog: Stillwoods.Blogspot.Ca
Author Blog: http://ghteed.blogspot.com/
Storefront: http://www.lulu.com/spotlight/lulubook22
Copyright © Doug Frizzle and/or Stillwoods, 2022.
Cover adapted from the original. Source files from University of Waterloo.

https://tinyurl.com/ve25d42s This link should go to a spreadsheet of all known Teed stories. The list is annotated with various information on the stories and my progress with recapturing the work. The library of Teed's stories increases almost weekly. Check at the Lulu.Com for the latest arrivals. Search for Teed./drf

Keywords: The Answers Library, Canadian Romance, 1917.
Cautionary Note: This series of books by Stillwoods are intended to make the stories of G. H. Teed, born in New Brunswick, Canada, available to collectors and researchers. The editor, or rather digitizer has not altered the original publication.

This story may contain language and racial terms that are not appropriate to today. I apologize for them; I know that the author was using his voice to excite and entertain an adventurous English audience. These works were published from 82 to 110 years ago. Most every work has characters of redeeming ethnicity within.

I hope you enjoy and share these stories; I have.
Doug Frizzle

With thanks to the University of Waterloo, Ontario, for providing scans of this magazine. /drf

A Fine Complete Canadian Romance!

This Grand Long Novel Deals with Life in Canada and England.
A Love Awakened; Or, The Cross Roads in Life. By the Author of "Yvonne". ILLUSTRATED BY J R BURGESS

This Grand Long Novel Deals with Life in Canada and England.

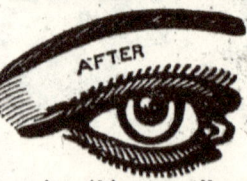

"I CANNOT face such a future, Dick."

As the words fell slowly, reluctantly, from the lips of the girl, she turned her serious hazel eyes away from the young fellow who sat on the log fence beside her, and gazed across the wide valley, where the river sparkled beneath the sun of New Brunswick's late spring. Both sides of the river were the same—wide, rolling country, sloping gently up from the banks of the St. John to low ridges—the richest farming country in the whole province. In sharp contrast against the green were the regular patches of cultivation just beginning to be touched by the faintest tinge of emerald where the newly planted crops were starting to reach upwards to the sun and warmth.

At intervals on both sides of the valley were the homesteads of the farmers—plain, primitive buildings were they, belonging to no school of architecture, except that crude one of necessity peculiar to the back blocks.

Up on the ridge a line of spruce and fir trees made a dark line against the clear blue of the sky. Here and there the paler green of the hackmatak showed vividly, and, straggling along the edge, were groves of white and yellow birch, their flimsy strips of bark fluttering like silver and topaz ribbons in the soft breeze which presaged the coming of summer.

Below, and still swelling from bank to bank with the spring flood from the headwaters, was the St. John River, mothering and enriching the fertile valley through which it flowed. Away to the north was a smudge against the blue sky which marked the position of Woodstock, the market town of the district. But to east and west and south were farms—farms—farms, as far as the eye could reach.

The fence on which the boy and girl sat was a rude, log, "snake" affair, built of spruce and fir, from which the bark had been stripped. It formed the boundary line between two of the farms, and that the young fellow belonged to one was evident, for, in the brown field on one side, where the newly turned soil was redolent of earthy smells, a pair of farm horses, hitched to a harrow, stood waiting for him to resume his work.

He was a clean-looking, upstanding young fellow, garbed in a manner typical of the district—a checked cotton shirt, stained blue overalls caught over the shoulders by blue braces, with the legs tucked into a pair of locally made Wellington boots. On his head was a soft hat, which, at the moment, was pushed back from his sweating brow, revealing a little of the close-cropped chestnut hair which crowned his head.

Although just past twenty years of age, he had already taken on the responsibilities and was doing the work of a man of thirty, for in the province of New Brunswick, as in the rest of Canada, life and its full meaning must be grappled with at an early age—particularly on the land.

He was neither handsome, nor ugly. Nor had life bitten sufficiently hard yet to leave its mark upon his features, and to indicate what sort of a father the boy would be to the man.

The girl was a year or so younger, though her hair still hung down her back in a thick ebony braid. Not even the coarse calico dress which she wore, and which was stamped with the crude lines of home manufacture, could hide the supple grace of her youthful body. She wore no hat, and the sun had free play with her features. Her face and throat were as brown as a berry, while her mouth was a deep crimson slash against the brown. Her eyes were serious, and well placed in her head. Her nose was straight and decisive, and her chin, though soft and round, was full of character.

But perhaps the best feature of her face was her brow, for it was low and broad—the brow of a thinker, the brow of one who must see and know, of one who could not accept life at second hand. Her feet were bare, almost as brown as the earth beneath, and the tiny, spreading toes showed not a blemish upon them.

They two, this girl and this boy, had come to the crossroads in life, where man and woman, on the threshold of the future and with the wine of Spring singing in their blood, have met throughout the ages. And it was in reply to the question, which had been Dick Saunders' challenge to fate, that the girl had spoken.

"I cannot face such a future, Dick," she repeated, after a long silence.

The young fellow twisted his toil-toughened hands helplessly.

"But—but, Eleanor," he stammered, while a wave of crimson crept slowly up beneath the tan, "I—I thought it was meant that you and I —"

Swiftly the girl turned to him, and laid one slender, russet-coloured hand on his soil-stained knee.

"Listen, Dick," she interrupted, "I know what you would say. Of course, it was meant that you and I should marry. It has been intended ever since we were children—intended by our parents; and it is but natural that you should have grown up to think the same. But that does not make it an accomplished fact. I cannot do it, Dick."

"But, Eleanor," he blurted out, like one who has been suddenly hurt by the hand which has always held a caress, "don't you—don't you like me?"

For a moment the girl's eyes closed, and her breast rose quickly. How could she say what she had to say while those puzzled, hurt, brown eyes were on her? It was only by keeping steadily before her the star to which she had hitched the waggon of her ambition that she was able to conquer the weakness which assailed her at that moment. The pain within her breast was her heart's reply to his halting question, a reply which she smothered before it found voice, for it must not tell him, as it told her, that she loved him with all the strength of the pulsing youth which surged within her. It was this moment which she had dreaded. It was this moment when Dick Saunders should ask her, as she knew he would ask her, to marry him, that she had been preparing her defences against for nearly two years.

The Saunders farm and the Hanington farm had adjoined each other for five generations, ever since the United Empire Loyalists had fled as refugees from the newly formed United States of America.

In the St. John River valley the Haningtons and the Saunders, in company with others, had formed a colony, and there, through generations, they had existed to the present day. Intermarriage had followed between the different families of the colony, and, side by side, Dick Saunders and Eleanor Hanington had grown up together, even as their ancestors had before them. In fact, through a marriage some two generations before, Dick Saunders was even distantly related to Eleanor Hanington. As they had grown from childhood into boyhood and girlhood, it had become to be taken for granted that when they reached maturity they should marry. Yet, although a close camaraderie had always existed between them, no word of love had been spoken until on this day, when Dick Saunders put his fate to the test.

His mother had died some years before, and two years later his father had followed her, leaving the farm to Dick. From the point of view of the farming community of the valley, there was no more eligible young man in the district than Dick Saunders. From a healthy-minded boy he had grown into a hard-working, far-seeing young man, who promised to do more for the Saunders farm than any of his ancestors had ever done.

Dick Saunders had never been content with the intermittent periods of education which had always been found good enough by the rest of the farming community. Perhaps it was Eleanor Hanington's example which had caused him to tramp the six miles through the snow in winter to the Woodstock High School, while other boys of the same age from the district were already having their first experience of the northern lumber camps.

Following that, he had gone to the capital city of Fredericton, to take a course in modern agriculture, and, had not the death of his father called him back to take charge of the farm, it had been his intention to go on to the provincial university. All of which goes to prove that Dick Saunders had the makings in him of a solid, substantial citizen—a man who should become a power in the district, and whom any girl in the community, with regard for a future without hazard, should be glad to marry.

Yet, strangely enough, here was Eleanor Hanington, the playmate of his childhood, the sweetheart of his boyhood days, and now looked upon in the valley as "his girl," telling him that she could not anticipate such a future.

"I am afraid you won't understand, Dick," she went on, "but I will tell you why it is impossible—now. Look, Dick. Look at the valley before you. You see farms on both sides of the river, which are called the richest farms in the province. Here, beneath us, is deep, rich soil, as good as any to be found. For five generations your people and my people have farmed this land. And where are we? What have we gained?

"We have scarcely more than our ancestors, who first came here a hundred and thirty-five years ago. Your family and mine have come down side by side, and only very occasionally is there the record of one having broken away to seek the outside world. All down the river and up the river you will find Haningtons and Saunders living the same life which we live. Our history is the history of the other families on the river.

"How many men, Dick, of the farms you can see from here have a balance in the bank? How many of their fathers or grandfathers before them made any money? How many of them have sought or been able to seek any of the wealth of culture which lies in the outside world? It is true that of recent years many young men have left the valley to seek an opening in the West, and, while the weaklings have returned, the others have not achieved, or we should have heard of them.

"Dick, it is hard for me to say, but even as a little girl something made me hate the whole cycle of life here. I did not mind the work. Spring, here in the valley, is an opening of paradise, Summer is languidly glorious, and the Autumn, with its Indian summer, makes me ache with its beauty." And she laid her hand on her breast as she spoke.

"But the long winters, Dick—the winters full of local gossip, which grows, oh, so stale—no, no, Dick, I cannot —I could not bear a lifetime of it. That is why, when we finished at the little school here, I insisted that I should be allowed to go to the high school at Woodstock. Then I had no definite aims in life, and if I thought of the future at all, it was with the vague understanding that you and I should live it together. Therefore I was determined that we should have interests a little deeper than those of the people about us. But the high school opened up such wonderful vistas to me, Dick. I joined the public library in the town, and read and read, drinking in information as a man in the desert, crazed with thirst, would drink up water.

"There was no one to guide my reading, and it is only natural that the knowledge I acquired should turn my mind into a chaos of impressions, sometimes vivid, sometimes blurred, but always increased my hunger to know more.

"I may be alien in thought to the rest of the community The other girls here are content to sit down to wait until the boys have had their fling in the towns and the lumber camps, then to marry and settle down to rear children, as their mothers have before them.

"Their literature is the local newspaper, their study of art extends to the coloured pictures of the almanacs and calendars which the Woodstock dealers give them. They are content to slave all day, season after season, year after year, creeping to bed at night worn out, and beginning a new day not rested. They grow old prematurely, and their children will follow the same round.

"There is nothing beyond. There is no height to inspire one with ambition to climb to its peak. If they must live this life, it is better that they remain in ignorance of the outside world and what it holds."

Suddenly the girl's arms went up, and she held them out towards the distant ridge, which, from the valley, was the horizon rim of beyond.

"Oh, Dick!" she cried, "beyond there somewhere is the world— the great world, which is full of pictures and books and people— things we have read of vaguely, but which beckon me with a strength I cannot resist. I, too, am only an ignorant girl of the valley. Look at me, Dick—look at me! A cheap calico dress which I made myself" — and she held the skirts out in dainty disdain. "Look at my feet, stained with the brown of the soil!"

"You look all right to me!" mumbled Dick.

She whirled on him suddenly.

"Yes, Dick, because your criterion is the valley. No, no, Dick. I—I cannot do it. I must see the outside world. I cannot anticipate a future of hand-to-mouth existence in the valley. I must go into the outside world. I can work, I shall work, and I shall study, oh, so hard! Then, perhaps, I could gain a little of the intellectual wealth I crave. Oh, Dick, Dick—"

Suddenly her voice broke, and, eyes swimming with tears, she turned and sped like a young fawn over the brown earth towards the farmhouse beyond.

Dick Saunders, slow-thinking, as were his ancestors, sat dumbly watching her as she went. Her words had come upon him with the suddenness of a summer thunderclap.

Never for a single moment had he guessed the ambition to which the last few years had given birth in her mind. Having grown up side by side with her, her loveliness did not strike him as it would have struck a stranger coming to the valley for the first time.

He only knew that, when he anticipated a future with her, a delightful pain stirred him inside, causing him to gaze out over the land with eyes full of calm content. Now, in a few startling moments, the girl he thought he knew so well had become an utter stranger to him. Her passionate cry of desire for intellectual richness had robbed him of all coherency of thought.

Dick's aim in going to high school and then on to the agricultural college had been to equip himself to become a better farmer—to make the Saunders' farm pay a reasonable profit for the time and labour which he should expend upon it. It had never occurred to him to seek more knowledge as an equipment to the battle of life outside the valley.

Now, on this warm day of late spring, when the smell of the humid brown earth made his nostrils twitch with the deep love of the soil which was ingrained in him, he found that the valley, which had always formed his criterion of the richness of God's gift to Nature, had suddenly grown grey, and chilled, and barren. He did not yet realise that it was the girl's presence which had edged the picture with a rosy tint.

Yet slowly, cumbrously, methodically, as was his wont, he pondered on her words even as he went slowly back to the horses, and, picking up the reins, took his seat on the disc harrow.

Up and down, up and down, during all the rest of the afternoon Dick Saunders drove his horses over the barren soil, mulching for the conservation of moisture, as he had been taught to do at the agricultural college. Yet it was his subconsciousness which guided the horses and lifted the discs when they turned. His every conscious sense was grappling with the problem which had so suddenly come into his life.

Unknown to himself, Dick Saunders had a depth of understanding which told him that Eleanor Hanington's words were not the cry of hysteria. It never occurred to him to think that by the morrow she would feel differently. He knew that to him, and to him only, had she uttered that soul cry. And he knew, too, that while conditions were as they were she would not marry him.

When evening came he busied himself about the chores around the homestead until the old woman who kept house for him called him to supper. He ate the meal in silence with the old woman and the boy who helped him on the farm, then, instead of strolling over to the Hanington place, as was his custom, he went out on the front porch and stuffed his corn-cob pipe with tobacco.

Ordinarily Dick Saunders was in bed not later than ten. But it was long after midnight on this occasion before he finally knocked the ashes from his pipe and went up the narrow staircase to his room.

The following morning was Wednesday, and instead of going about the work of the farm as usual, Dick Saunders hitched up one of the horses to the buggy and started off for Woodstock, a most unheard-of thing in the valley, where it was the general custom to go to town on Saturday.

Reaching the town, he drove down the steep hill of the main street past the Carlyle Hotel, and pulled up just before he got to the bridge in front of Judge Dibble's office.

Judge Dibble had always attended to the few legal matters which had cropped up during the lifetime of Dick's father and grandfather; therefore he went to the old judge as a matter of course. Judge Dibble was in his office, his feet cocked up on an antiquated desk, with a copy of the local paper on his knees, and occupied, while he read, in spitting tobacco-juice with marvellous precision into a sawdust-filled box some six feet distant.

"'Lo, Dick!" he grunted, as Dick walked in. "What brings you to town on a Wednesday?"

Dick Saunders laid his hat on the desk and drew up a chair before speaking.

"Judge Dibble, I want you to sell my farm for me."

It needed a good deal to jar the old judge out of his customary habit of repose, but Dick Saunders' calm statement succeeded in doing so. The paper fell to the floor, and his feet came down with a crash, while he bent forward and looked with kindly old eyes at the boy.

"What's that you say, Dick?"

"I want you to sell my farm for me, judge."

"Sell your farm! Sell the Saunders' farm!" exclaimed the judge, as one trying to understand the incomprehensible. "Why, you bain't going away, be you, Dick?" he went on, dropping into the vernacular of the district. "A Saunders has been on that there farm since New Brunswick was a howling wilderness, Dick; and you're the last of the lot. I was expecting you to come in, Dick, to see me about you and the little Hanington girl gittin' hitched up into double harness. What's the matter, boy?"

"Nothing, judge," responded Dick, with a suspicious gulp; "at least, I can't tell even you."

"You bain't been doing nothing wrong, boy; I know that."

Dick shook his head.

"Will you sell it for me, judge?" he persisted.

"Well, I reckon that won't be hard, Dick, if you really mean what you say. Better go back home and think it over. Come and see me again on Saturday, and we'll talk then."

"My mind is made up, judge. I want to sell, and as quick as

possible."

"There never was no use arguing with a Saunders once he had his mind set on a thing," mumbled the judge, as he reached behind him and picked up a deed box. "Well, let's see, Dick, you've got about two hundred acres there, haven't you?"

"Two hundred and thirty, judge."

"What's the least you'll take for it?"

"Well, judge, the Fisher place, which hadn't as good soil as mine, fetched eighty dollars an acre. I'd take that, and even seventy dollars, for a quick sale."

"How much stock have you got on it, Dick?".

"Four draught horses, two light horses, six cows, and some pigs."

"Do you want to sell them, too?"

"I want to sell everything—lock, stock, and barrel, judge."

"You're quite sure you don't want to tell me what's made you come to this decision, Dick?"

"I'd like to, judge, but—I can't."

The old man sighed, for he liked the boy, and was afraid that some trouble had come upon him which he was grappling with in the wrong way.

"All right, Dick," he said. "Go home, and I'll see what I can do."

"You'll push it along, judge, won't you?" said Dick, as he rose.

The old man nodded.

"I'll go at it at once, Dick; but, all the same, I think you're a blamed young fool. Yours is about the only farm in the valley without a mortgage on it, and you ought to do well there. I was in hopes, after you came back from the agricultural college, you'd shake them up a bit in the valley, and—"

But there the judge broke off, for Dick had gone, and there was little satisfaction in talking at a wooden door.

Judge Dibble found little difficulty in discovering a purchaser for the Saunders' farm, and while part of the money had to be financed through the bank, it was just a week later that Dick Saunders left the land of his fathers, and, without a glance in the direction of the Hanington place, drove to Woodstock, where he caught the night train for Montreal. But he was to have one more sight of the valley, for, as the train sped southwards to pick up the Montreal express at McAdam Junction, its course took it along the ridge which was the valley's rim of beyond.

And as he gazed out upon the green and brown slopes, tinged with the lambent hues of the setting sun, a mist filled his eyes, but he clenched his hands, and muttered over and over again:

"I've got twenty thousand dollars, and I'll make good. Then I'll come back and get her."

The smoke from the train was but a sable plume against the pale mauve of the evening sky when, from the Hanington homestead, a girl, bare-footed and clad in a red calico dress, sped through the sloping fields at the back of the house until she came to a paddock of young clover. There she threw herself face downwards, and, with breast heaving against the still warm earth, with slender, brown fingers unconsciously crushing the sweet young clover, she gave herself up to a paroxysm of remorse, while a virginal young moon came up over the ridge and watched her grief.

CHAPTER I. *Five Years Later.*

RICHARD SAUNDERS hung up the receiver of his desk telephone, and sat drumming restlessly on the arm of his chair. The conversation he had just finished had not, apparently, been of a very satisfactory nature, if one were to judge by the cloud of concentration which darkened his eyes.

It is a far cry from the sphere of a farm-lad on a back blocks farm in New Brunswick to that of a powerful wheat operator in London, and, despite the fact that cases of achievement from obscurity to opulence are common enough, it is not often that a gap of such magnitude is bridged in five short years. Yet Richard Saunders had brought a considerable measure of achievement into that period of time, and few men could show a more consistent record of advance than he.

A little over five years before Dick Saunders had known little beyond the narrow confines of the back-woods valley in which he had been born and reared.

At the very moment when any change from the existing order of things had been undreamed of by him, a crisis had developed in his life, which, by the very force of the upheaval it had caused, had hurled him out of the quiet backwater where he had been resting into the rush and hurly-burly of the great world beyond. The only visible cause for Dick Saunders' uprooting of the influence and conventional objectives instilled through generations of pioneering ancestors had been the soul cry of a slip of a girl, who, nevertheless, had held Dick Saunders' destiny in the hollow of her hand. Through the cumbrous workings of his mind her words had probed with the inevitable certainty of steel shafts, though it is impossible that she herself could have foreseen the dramatic upheaval they were to cause.

After his memorable interview with Eleanor Hanington, when the girl, filled with the hunger of a starved soul, had cried out in an agony of desire for the Unknown, and what it might hold, Dick Saunders had started out to pit himself, as thousands before him, against the Titan which controls the destinies of men.

Arriving in Montreal, it had been a small thing which had sent him West, but the rumour which had given him his first lead had paid dividends over and over again, for in the West Dick Saunders had found the road by which he would achieve ultimate realisation.

With the land boom climbing to its zenith, he had quadrupled the capital he had taken with him, and then, with a kindly fate still guiding his actions, he had invested every available penny in wheat at a time when the crop prospects had been very uncertain.

Once again luck had been with him, and with scarcely a single setback he had marched steadily onwards to a position where he was known as one of the biggest wheat operators in the West.

It is, perhaps, not unnatural that, while the remembrance of Eleanor Hanington was still strong within him, the vision he had carried in his heart had been clouded to some extent by the passage of time and the rush of affairs. If he had achieved to some extent, Dick Saunders had not done it without falling a victim to that insidious disease which is a natural corollary to material success—ambition.

Gradually, but, nevertheless, insistently, a still greater world had called him, and with a record of extraordinary success behind him, Dick Saunders had started for London, to seek there even wider achievement.

It was with the feeling of confidence and security he had broken his journey at Montreal to go down into New Brunswick to find the girl he had left there on a backwoods farm. But if Dick Saunders' life had seen radical changes, so had the place he still pictured in his mind as a quiet, rural backwater, with the broad river flowing through its heart, for scarcely had Dick Saunders been gone eighteen months when, as in a great many other places in the country, rich oil deposits had been discovered.

Farms which for generations had paid a bare living, but which, nevertheless, had retained the pristine loveliness of nature, were now disfigured with huge derricks, and the once green slopes of the valley were now blackened and desolate from the deadly clutch of oil. But those who had once farmed the valley land recked not of the abomination of desolation which had stretched its fingers broadcast. They had found a potent salve in the fortunes which had descended upon them with dramatic suddenness, and it was through this derrick-ridden country that Dick Saunders came back to seek Eleanor Hanington. But, in common with the rest of the valley, the Hanington farm lay beneath the shadow of a huge, spindly derrick, and there were none to tell him what had become of the Haningtons.

All he could gather was that, shortly after his own departure from the valley, old man Hanington had died. Then had followed the discovery of oil, and, like the other landowners in the district, the Haningtons had leaned into sudden opulence. Shortly after, so he was told, Eleanor Hanington and her mother had gone away, but their correspondence had been of the most fitful nature, and for over a year no word of any description had come from them.

It was the first real disappointment Dick Saunders had had during the three years of his own rapid climb to wealth, and as he departed from the home of his youth, for the second time, he once more registered a vow. Before he had sworn that he would return and claim the girl whose passionate words had inspired his departure. He had kept his promise; but now, as the express carried him swiftly on towards Montreal, he vowed that in even greater activity he would find forgetfulness.

So two more years had passed—two years during which the same extraordinary luck pursued him, and made him one of the most powerful wheat operators in Europe.

It was at this point in his career, however, that Dick Saunders began to discover the fickleness of Dame Fortune. With an almost uncanny foresight he had bought or sold vast quantities of wheat during the past two years, and as he became decidedly a factor to be reckoned with in the world of big business, he gradually got to be known as "the man who never made a mistake!"

Nor did the world at large guess for a single moment that at this very time Dick Saunders had plunged more heavily than ever into a huge speculation in wheat, and that, for the first time in five years, he had been caught napping.

Convinced that the world crop prospects foreshadowed huge supplies of new wheat for the coming season, he had gone short heavily on the market, expecting to make his deliveries when the new wheat should come in, and when he would be able to buy at a far cheaper price than he had paid. Only recently, however, had Dick Saunders discovered the existence of powerful opposition in the market—opposition he had traced to a strong financial group, at the head of which was a man against whom he had been pitted on more than one occasion during the preceding two years.

For some time past Saunders had become aware that all his own sales of wheat were being snapped up in the same quarter, but only during the last three days had he begun to realise that he had walked into one of the most Machiavellian traps which had ever been laid for an unwary market operator.

His mistake had been in counting on only ordinary market competition as a possible contingency against the success of his campaign. He knew now, however, that from the first moment his scheme had been launched he had been the objective of a definite counter-campaign— a campaign which had been initiated for the sole purpose of ruining him. A man like Saunders—a man who two years before had been utterly unknown—could not rise to such a position of power without at the same time creating powerful enemies.

With the supreme belief in his own abilities, Saunders had gone forward, not indifferently, but with confidence that he could take care of himself, and it was with something of a shock that he now realised he had been caught napping badly. It was not, however, until only a short week lay between him and the time when he must make the first deliveries against the sales he had contracted that the persistency with which he failed to acquire stocks told him there was something in existence as a factor which was of a far more serious nature than a natural shortage of wheat stocks.

His first deliveries were to be made on the following Monday, and during that week he had almost lived on the telephone, hammering at his brokers continually, and following up every possible channel which seemed likely to have wheat at the end of it. But now, on the Saturday, he realised that he was still short of nearly half the amount he must deliver on Monday.

It was not that the stocks of wheat did not exist in the country. His inquiries had assured him that he could buy the quantity he needed—at a price. These supplies, however, he had discovered were under the control of the powerful ring with which his own sales had been contracted, and the position was simply that, in order to make delivery, he would be compelled to purchase the amount he was short from the very source to which he had sold, and which he knew, beyond the shadow of a doubt, was plotting his ruin.

His brokers had put out tentative feelers to ascertain at which price the ring was holding the wheat, and the figure that they had passed on to Dick Saunders told him that to purchase for delivery at that price would mean stark and swift ruin.

Nor did there seem any solution of the matter. Bitterly he reproached himself for plunging so heavily without a greater regard for his lines of communication, so to speak. Up to the very last moment of Saturday's market he had striven desperately to locate supplies of wheat, even small lots held outside the ring which was fighting him. But all to no purpose. Cables from Russia, Canada, Australia, the United States, and the Argentine, had been abortive of any suggestion to solve the problem which confronted him.

From each one of those countries there were cargoes of wheat on the way to England, but in every single instance was the grain the property of the enemy. Now, with the week-end ahead of him, he could do little, and if he should find no solution of the difficulty before three o'clock on Monday, he knew that all his contracts would be called, and that he must make default.

Even were he to throw his whole fortune into the breach it would avail nothing, for with the enemy in a position to name his own price on supplies, every penny he possessed would be swept away. They had him on the hip, and although, as he left his office that day, he betrayed no outward sign of his anxiety, Dick Saunders knew that, unless some miracle occurred, only forty-eight hours lay between him and utter financial ruin.

As he entered his car, and drove from the City to the Albany, in Piccadilly, where he had his chambers, Dick Saunders' mind was not altogether filled with the business side of his impending crash. There were other elements to be considered—elements which he knew must be faced over the week-end, and from which he flinched far more than from any factor in the affair which made it a personal question.

Dick Saunders had not only climbed high in the world of finance, but it was inevitable that a man of such mental calibre should have been acceptable in a social way. About him there was nothing uncouth, nor indicative of the parvenu. His manner was restrained and quiet, his appearance eminently correct, and his conversation always applied to the needs of the occasion. And if the three years he had spent in the West had chilled a little the vision he had carried in his heart of Eleanor Hanington, it is not unnatural; nor does it reflect in any degree upon the man's constancy that, after five years of silence, he should have found in the multitudes about him one who filled him, if not with the hectic passion of twenty, at least with a deep regard, which, through his own receptiveness of mood, the conventional acquiescence of the girl, and the careful nurturing of a far-seeing mother, had resulted in the inevitable.

It was now less than three months since Dick Saunders'

engagement to Dorothy Brett had been announced, and, even through the incessant demands of the new campaign upon which he had embarked, Saunders had never for a single moment neglected attending to the little superficialities which are naturally concomitant to such a state.

Dorothy Brett was typical of the class to which she belonged. Carefully nurtured, brought up in the strict convention of an upper middle-class family, educated according to the accepted tenets of her order, with a finishing course on the Continent, she was, with a natural shallowness of mind, hedged in by the narrow precepts of her class, the direct antithesis of Eleanor Hanington.

The one had been virile, and with a depth of character which, even on the threshold of womanhood, had found passionate expression. The other's whole existence was an exact replica of thousands like her, who were but the echo of the convention which had bred them; and yet it is not surprising that, in taking such a step, the one whom he had been fated to choose should have been so utterly different from the ideal which had filled his heart five years before, whose memory was clouded, as he thought, forgotten, but who had left an impression upon his soul which Dick Saunders was to find could never be erased.

It was the thought of Dorothy Brett which caused him to flinch, as he faced the week-end. He was due at the Brett place in Surrey that evening, to remain until Monday morning, and he knew that, during that time, he would have to make some attempt to explain to Dorothy the meaning of the ruin which was lying in wait for him.

If he had given any great thought to it at all, it had been to feel a sharp regret that they must face the future together under such circumstances. It had been one of his keenest pleasures to anticipate the happiness his wealth would bring her, and, to do him justice, it was because she would have to wait for these things, and not because he himself felt any fear of the future, that he dreaded the explanation.

He was already preparing his words to meet the needs of the occasion as he drove his car out of the courtyard of the Albany, and turned up Piccadilly on his way to the country. But during the hour and a half it took him to drive through to the Brett place, he had rejected form after form of opening, and, as he turned into the long drive which led up to the house, he dismissed the effort with a shrug. He could only leave the matter to circumstance, and fit his words to the demand of situation.

Little did he dream that, before that day had run its allotted course, he was to receive a far greater shock than had followed the discovery of the market plot against him.

GIVEN BACK TO HER LOVER!

Eleanor started back with a cry as she saw Dick Saunders sitting in the corner of the taxi. "Digby, this must not be," she cried. Falkiner thrust her inside and slammed the door.

CHAPTER II.   *A Heavy Blow is Followed by an Unexpected Meeting.*

BUT, surely, Richard, you cannot mean that we should be actually poor?"

"I am afraid I do, Dorothy," rejoined Dick Saunders, professing a cheerfulness he by no means felt.

"But why, Richard?" she exclaimed. "I do not understand. I thought you had plenty of money."

"You would scarcely comprehend the details," he rejoined slowly. "But it is because I have plunged heavily into certain wheat speculations, which have not developed as I expected."

"But surely that does not mean that your whole fortune is at stake, Richard?"

"It means more than that. Let me explain, Dorothy. In the first place, you know that my business is dealing in wheat, and I base my actions against the probabilities of supply and demand. In anticipating these factors, I have never before made a serious mistake, nor have I made one in that direction on this occasion.

"The present difficulty, however, has been caused through my own negligence, for not until too late did I discover there were powerful forces arrayed against me. During the past three months I have contracted large sales of wheat, which I anticipated I should be able to deliver on certain dates. The first of these deliveries is to be made on Monday, and about two weeks ago, with the market price far lower than when I had made my sales, I began to make the necessary purchases for delivery. But when I had collected less than half the quantity required I suddenly discovered that it was impossible to get hold of further stocks. It was then I realised the market had been swept bare by other buyers, and when I had ferreted it out, I ascertained that these buyers were the very persons to whom I myself had contracted to make delivery. I could have bought from them the necessary quantity which I would have to deliver back to them, but, having cornered all the grain at present available in the country, they could place, and did place, such a prohibitive price upon it that, if I purchased from them, it meant utter ruin. On the other hand, if I did not make delivery, and I cannot make delivery, on Monday, it also means ruin. So that is the matter in a nutshell, Dorothy."

They were seated on a bench in a small arbour which nestled in one corner of the garden, and Dick Saunders had found opportunity less than an hour after his arrival to get Dorothy Brett away from the others, and to tell her what was threatening.

The Bretts were giving a house-party over the weekend, and in the distance they could hear where they were sitting the laughing voices of the others who were gathered round the tea-table, which had been laid on the terrace.

Dick Saunders, had motored down from town intentionally early in order to be there before the other guests should arrive, and it was just as he was descending from his room that he had come upon Dorothy on her way to the terrace.

Her greeting had been affectionate enough, but so engrossed was he in endeavouring to explain the meaning of the disaster which loomed up ahead that Dick Saunders had not yet seen the sudden stiffness of her figure, the almost imperceptible drawing away from him as he spoke.

Dorothy Brett was like thousands of other girls of her class. Saunders, a man eminently eligible as a husband from the material point of view, had been swept into the activities of Dorothy's far-seeing mother, and almost before he knew what was happening he had found himself the girl's accepted suitor. Never for a single moment did Saunders guess that his engagement to Dorothy Brett was other than his own making.

Mrs. Brett was a past-master in the social game, and so cunningly had she played her cards that the necessary propinquity had eventuated. To the girl herself the engagement had come as a matter of conventional course. Had she possessed more depth of character, it is just possible that her affection would have been placed elsewhere; but the only rival whom Saunders had had to contend with had been a boy just down from university, and whom Mrs. Brett had easily disposed of. Then, with a free running, Saunders had done exactly what had been expected of him. Nor did it occur to him that, without the fortune he was reputed to possess he would not for a single moment have been persona grata with Mrs. Brett.

Saunders' money had been sufficient to dull any natural regrets which either Dorothy or her mother may have had that Dick Saunders was not English, and under this influence it was easily forgotten that he was a Colonial. These considerations, however, were utterly beyond Dick's conception of the scheme of things, and, therefore, while he was blind to the attitude Dorothy was adopting, it needed the words which she spoke a little later to enlighten him.

It is unlikely that she grasped to any extent the details of the conversation which had arisen. She had taken in only the major facts of the matter, and, unless Dick Saunders were joking, then she realised that she must look upon him as a penniless suitor, which vastly altered the objective she had held.

She was not unwilling that he should continue to explain matters, and while she made no attempt to understand the cause, she had already considered the effect, and now, as his voice droned on, her mind was working rapidly towards a point of decision.

It was when he had finished, and, turning, had taken her hand, saying as he did so, "So you see, Dorothy, the exact position of things. It means that you must wait for a little, and that then we must fight upwards together," that gently, but, nevertheless, insistently, she withdrew her fingers from his grasp.

"Surely you are joking, Richard!" she said slowly. "A week ago there was no sign of anything like this, and now, without the slightest warning, you tell me that you are ruined. Is there no way we can evade it?"

Saunders glanced at her searchingly. There was a chill in her words, which had acted upon him like a cold douche. But, realising what a shock the news must have been to her, he told himself that her attitude was but natural under the circumstances.

"I am afraid you do not understand, Richard," she went on, after a short pause. "You do not seem to grasp my position. When our engagement was announced it was but natural that all our friends should know about you. Now, how can I go to them and say that we have nothing, that we should start our married life as paupers? Even if I were willing to do so, dear mamma would never consent. And then think of the publicity, Richard, if you are coming a cropper! Everyone will know it, and that sort of notoriety I could never stand."

"But I thought you were fond of me, Dorothy?" he exclaimed.

The girl shrugged.

"Don't be ridiculous, Richard!" she said. "Of course I am fond of you, otherwise I should not have contemplated marrying you. I feel deeply for you, too, in this trouble which has come upon you; but don't you think it is a little too much for you to expect that I should marry you under those conditions?"

21

"I am afraid I did not look at it in that way, Dorothy," answered Dick Saunders slowly. "I came to you to tell you as soon as I knew, and perhaps, as you say, I was selfish in thinking only of myself."

"The point for us to consider," she broke in, "is what we must do. I suppose, Richard, you have neglected nothing that would furnish a solution of the trouble, and you cannot be joking upon such a serious matter."

"I am not joking, nor have I neglected a single channel which offered hope," he responded. "It was only when everything had failed that I came to you. Unless a miracle happens between now and Monday, then I shall have to make default, which means exactly what I said."

"But don't you see what a terrible position this puts me in?" she cried. "Can't you understand what a laughing-stock I shall be? I know I shall die of shame! And yet you calmly sit there and show no consideration for me. How can I possibly get through the week-end with this thing hanging over my head?"

"I am sorry it has upset you so, and that you have taken it in this way," remarked Saunders heavily. "I should have waited until Sunday night or Monday morning before I told you."

Abruptly Dorothy got to her feet.

"Richard," she said, "we will say nothing more about this until Monday morning. I may be compelled to tell dear mamma, in order that she shall refrain from saying too much to our quests. In the meantime, you must try to find a way out, and, if you should succeed, then things shall be the same as before. If not—"

And she finished her remark with a shrug.

As Dick Saunders stood and watched her pass out of the arbour, his mind became filled with chaotic thoughts. For the moment he had forgotten his financial troubles, and was struggling desperately to understand the meaning of the girl's amazing attitude.

But as he fought his fight alone there in the arbour he began gradually to realise the truth, and with realisation came a searching of his own soul. It seemed impossible that at the moment he could follow Dorothy and mix with the other guests, yet he knew that until Monday, for his own sake as well as for hers, he must play the part. Summoning all his will-power to his assistance, he threw back his shoulders, and, with no outward sign of the seething chaos within, he strode forth to join the others.

22

It was just when he had emerged from the arbour that, on the lawn ahead of him, he saw Dorothy talking to a girl, who had evidently just arrived. His inclination was to turn off along another path, but, realising that they had both seen him, he made his way to where they were standing, and with a gaiety and lightness of manner which gave no hint of their recent discussion, Dorothy called to him.

As he drew nearer, Dick Saunders glanced at the girl whose arm was intertwined with Dorothy's; then, as his eyes fell upon her, the mask of politeness which had rested on his countenance was suddenly torn asunder, and for one fleeting second he gazed at her in stark amazement.

As for the girl, she had already heard enough from Dorothy to forewarn her, and in her manner there was no suggestion of the emotion which had surged up within her, and had suffused her senses to the verge of faintness.

By a superhuman effort Dick Saunders recovered himself, and, feeling inwardly thankful that Dorothy had not noticed the discomposure he had exhibited, and, when a moment later he was introduced to Eleanor Hanington, he bowed with a degree of polite restraint which hid absolutely the panic of his mind.

Like a bolt from the blue the incredible had happened. In one brief instant the mist of five years had been rent asunder, and as the eyes of those two leaped towards each other they saw, not with the understanding of the present, but with the vision which had been theirs five years before.

From Dick Saunders the picture of that quiet English garden faded away, and instead of the two girls garbed according to the latest dictates of fashion, he saw but one—a barefooted girl, in a crudely cut calico dress, with sun-tanned skin and wind-blown hair.

Before him rose the picture of the rough log bench upon which they two had sat, and then with lightning swiftness he visualised the dramatic appeal the girl had made to Fate. As suddenly as the vision had come so did it pass, and the next moment he was muttering some conventional remark to the new Eleanor Hanington.

For some reason she had chosen to suppress any remark about the past, and, taking his cue from her, Dick Saunders said nothing; but if, before, his mind had been chaos, it was now a seething maelstrom as they turned and crossed the lawn towards the terrace.

Only by the conversation between the two girls was he able to discover that their friendship had begun at the same school in Paris, and that Eleanor Hanington's arrival that afternoon was the result of a long-promised visit. Yet, if she retained any real remembrance of five years before, she gave no sign, nor, since that one tense glance which had bridged the canyon of time, did her eyes reveal aught but a cool, impersonal interest in Dick Saunders.

They were still some distance from the terrace, when Dick saw a man detach himself from the crowd round the tea-table and come towards them. There was something vaguely familiar about him, and as he drew still nearer Saunders caught his breath sharply, for in him he recognised none other than Digby Falkiner, the man who dominated the powerful ring which was out to break him.

Not until that moment had Saunders known that Falkiner was to be a member of the house-party, yet his control, although severely shaken by the events of the day, did not desert him as they met. Falkiner himself a man verging on forty, and who, through strenuous years of market operations, had developed the impassive mask of a gambler, greeted the two girls, then turned to Saunders, and bowed with a casual manner which gave no hint of what lay between them. Then—just how it was managed Dick Saunders scarcely knew—but suddenly he found himself standing alone with Dorothy, while Digby Falkiner had appropriated Eleanor Hanington, and was coolly leading her towards the arbour.

He stood gazing after them with a dull pain hammering at his heart, then Dorothy's voice recalled him, and, turning with a muttered apology, he accompanied her on to the terrace.

CHAPTER III. *Eleanor Hanington Makes a Strange Bargain.*

IT was long past twelve that night before Dorothy Brett and Eleanor Hanington found an opportunity for those girlish confidences which were natural after more than a year's separation. Utterly unlike in every way, it is strange that they should have grown to such intimacy; but in the Bretts Eleanor Hanington had found a wealth of kindness and hospitality which had filled her with gratitude, while in her Dorothy had discovered a strength of character and a staunchness that had been her sheet-anchor when at school.

As usual, it was she who talked and Eleanor Hanington who listened. They were sitting on the bed in Eleanor's room, and it was not unnatural that Eleanor's first question should have been about Dick Saunders. It was only when Dorothy, without the slightest warning, threw herself down sobbing that Eleanor Hanington gathered that all was not well. While she soothed the other she listened to the story, and when Dorothy's voice had whimpered off into silence Eleanor tightened her arms about the girl's shoulders, and said:

"But, Dorothy dear, it doesn't really matter if you love him. If he is in difficulties in business it does not mean the end of everything. He is young, and you are young, and if he has fought his way up once he can do it again. It will mean waiting a little while, but, after all, what does that matter? If you look at it in that way, darling, you will see it is not half as bad as you think. You are upset to-night, but in the morning I am sure you will see it differently."

"Never! I shall never be able to face my friends," wailed Dorothy. "Think of the gossip there will be! I shall be the laughing-stock of everyone. I shall die of shame, I know I shall!"

"There is no shame in failure," said Eleanor soothingly. "If Mr. Saunders has made a mistake in his business calculations, then he will have to start again, that is all. You are making too much of a tragedy of it, Dorothy."

"You do not understand, Eleanor. It is terrible. Richard himself says so, and dear mamma, she would never permit me to marry him if he had nothing. Besides, I myself could never face it. It was really too bad of Richard to allow himself to get into difficulties. Think of how I shall feel when the engagement is broken, and when everyone knows he is ruined."

"Don't you think you are considering only how it will affect you?" said Eleanor. "Don't you think it is going to be hard for him as well?"

"He is a man, and it is different," responded Dorothy querulously. "He should have thought of me and my position and friends before embarking upon an affair which held any chance of disaster."

"Did he tell you any details of the trouble?" asked Eleanor.

"Oh, it is something about buying or selling wheat. I did not pay much attention to that part of it. I could only realise the awful gossip that must follow."

Even with a full realisation of the weaknesses of Dorothy's character, Eleanor Hanington could not help but feel, in failing to grasp any of the details of Dick Saunders' story, the other had revealed a selfishness of outlook, a consideration for only how it should affect her, that was un-worthy, and it was because she wanted to see the girl rise to a real conception of womanhood that she fought that night to bring understanding to Dorothy, while her own heart was contracted with pain.

"Listen, darling," she said, as she softly stroked Dorothy's hair, "you are too upset to consider the matter calmly to-night. Go to Mr. Saunders to-morrow and talk it over again. Perhaps you will then find it is really not quite so bad as you think; and if there is no disgrace then it can't really matter what your friends say. Those who are worthy will honour you for waiting until he is on his feet again, and the others don't count. Perhaps, too, a way can be found out."

But Dorothy shook her head. If her nature was shallow, she had, nevertheless, a degree of obstinacy which was bolstered up by her petty fear and selfishness, and she made no secret to herself that Dick Saunders without money lacked the attraction as a husband which was a necessary corollary to the social ambitions which had been instilled in her from childhood.

"You do not understand," she wailed. "If Richard has lost all his money, then we can never be married, and even then I do not see how I am going to face the scandal."

Eleanor Hanington bent closer to the other.

"Tell me, Dorothy, do you love Mr. Saunders?"

"Of course I love him," she cried peevishly, "otherwise why should I be engaged to him? I thought him so strong, so splendid— like a rock; but how can I help being upset when I discover he has been so careless?"

Eleanor Hanington said nothing. Gazing straight ahead of her, she allowed her mind to go back five years to the day when she herself had refused the thing her whole nature had been yearning for ever since. Now she possessed all that she had cried out for in those days, which seemed an eternity away. To meet Dick Saunders, to feel the touch of his hand, and to look into his eyes, had brought back the old longing with redoubled force; but in the loyalty of her nature there was no room for any consideration of self. Through her Dorothy would never know what Dick Saunders had been to her. If he had forgotten, and if he loved Dorothy, then, if she could achieve it, she would prevent a wreckage of their lives.

Sitting there on the bed, mechanically stroking the other's hair, Eleanor Hanington fought out the struggle with herself, and when she had emerged from it she had buried deep within her soul the ache which she could control, but not forget. It was then, too, that, inspired by certain words of Dorothy's, her mind went back to her conversation with Digby Falkiner that afternoon, and suddenly words he had uttered held for her a definite meaning, and provided her with a plan which, even though it would be the road of torture for herself, might bring happiness to Dorothy Brett. And because she knew she must think, and think desperately, Eleanor said:

"Come to bed now, darling, and get some sleep. To-morrow we will find a way out. Don't worry any more."

Dorothy stumbled to her feet, and, with one arm about her, Eleanor went along to the other's room.

On returning to her own she turned out the light, and sat by the open window until far into the morning. She did not appear at breakfast, but afterwards, while the energetic ones were discussing church, she approached Digby Falkiner, and a moment later Dick Saunders saw them strolling off in the direction of the arbour. If Digby Falkiner felt any curiosity as to why Eleanor Hanington had taken him off, he did not show it. Ever since he had met her two years before he had loved her desperately, and it had been the biggest losing fight of his life that he had failed to win her love in return.

Just inside the arbour he stood, with head courteously inclined, waiting for her to speak, never guessing the momentous words which she was to utter, and on her part Eleanor Hanington was seized with a sudden panic, which almost made her falter in her purpose. Then, summoning all her determination, she began to speak:

"Mr. Falkiner," she faltered, "on more than one occasion you have done me the honour to ask me to marry you. I—I have never felt that I wished to give up my freedom, but since yesterday I have changed my mind, and if you still wish me, I—"

As she stammered with embarrassment, Digby Falkiner stepped forward swiftly and took her hand.

"Are you trying to tell me, Eleanor, that you will marry me?" he asked tensely.

"Yes," she whispered. "If you will have me under certain conditions."

"I will have you under any conditions," he said. "It is but for you to make them."

She laid one hand on his arm.

"Yesterday, when you were speaking to me, you said that there was one guest here who would probably find your presence unwelcome."

Digby Falkiner nodded.

"That is quite so," he rejoined.

"Would you—would you tell me his name, please?"

"Certainly, Eleanor. It is Saunders."

"And is it true that unless he can meet certain engagements to-morrow he will be ruined?"

"I am afraid it is, Eleanor. It was a fair fight, but Saunders was caught napping."

"Is it you who hold his destiny in your hand?"

"If he defaults to-morrow in the contracts he has made with me, he will break," responded Falkiner. "Is that what you mean?"

"Yes," she rejoined in a low tone. "And if you did not press him—if you gave him time, could he escape this crash which threatens him?"

"If I gave him a month he could."

"Then listen, Digby," she said. "Ever since I first came to England, five years ago, the Bretts have overwhelmed me with kindness. I feel towards them a debt of gratitude which I can never repay. You must know that Dorothy was to be married to Mr. Saunders, and last night she came to me very unhappy. Mr. Saunders had told her the ruin that threatened, and Dorothy cannot face the gossip she fears will follow. If he crashes to-morrow, it means that their whole future is wrecked. If it is in your power to save him by withdrawing your demands, then—then, Digby, I want you to do this thing for me. If you do you may ask me anything you will."

"You mean, Eleanor, that you will marry me?'

"Yes," she whispered.

"Then I will do as you ask. I shall tell Saunders to-day that I do not require delivery for another month."

"Oh, thank you," she cried brokenly.

And then, because Digby Falkiner had a marvellous depth of understanding, he did not do as a younger man might have done, but instead he gently took her arm and led her out of the arbour.

Half an hour later, with a cigar in the corner of his mouth, he strolled across the terrace to where Dick Saunders was standing gazing moodily out over the park. Saunders turned frowningly as Falkiner approached, but before he could speak Digby Falkiner said casually:

"Oh, by the way, Saunders, I meant to tell you that you can extend those contracts for a month if it is not quite convenient for you to make delivery to-morrow." And before the dumbfounded Dick Saunders could reply Falkiner was on his way back to the house.

THE MEETING IN ENGLAND.

"Have you for-gotten," cried Dick, "that it was you, with your cry for freedom, your desire for the out-side world, who sent me away?" Eleanor knew then that he loved her still. But she could do nothing. They never could be lovers again.

CHAPTER IV. *Dick Saunders is Puzzled.*

IF Dick Saunders had not known Digby Falkiner was not the type of man to indulge in practical jokes he would have thought there was something of the sort behind the amazing words he had just heard. But while he had never before met Falkiner personally, he knew sufficient about his record as a market operator to realise that in making the statement he had just made he had meant every word of it.

But why? That was what puzzled Dick Saunders. There was nothing of the sentimentalist about Digby Falkiner, and Saunders was in possession of sufficient information to feel absolutely certain that Falkiner and the ring he controlled had started out with the definite intention of breaking him.

It is indicative, too, of Dick Saunders' nature that, no sooner had he recovered from the first shock of surprise than he thought of Dorothy and how it would affect her. Yet, strangely enough, his heart did not leap within him at the thought, nor did he experience that upsurging of joy which should have been his portion. He was too loyal to permit himself to analyse this sudden coldness of spirit, and, keeping before him the single thought that now Dorothy would have nothing to fear, he turned and walked along the terrace towards the house to seek her. It was just then that Dorothy herself appeared, and, spying him on the terrace, waved, he went towards her, and as he drew near she smiled at him tenderly.

"Come along to the arbour, Dick," she said, appropriating his arm. "I have something to say to you."

"And I to you," he rejoined, matching the lightness of her tone.

Crossing the lawn, they passed between the two yew trees which guarded the entrance to the arbour. Then, when they were inside, Dorothy turned swiftly, and, laying a hand on each shoulder, said:

"Dick dear, I am sorry for acting as I did yesterday, but I was upset, and scarcely knew what I was saying. I want you to forget all about it, and it doesn't matter if you do lose all your money to-morrow. I will wait for you until you get another start."

Dick reached up, and, taking her hands in his, looked deep into her eyes.

"Do you mean that, Dorothy?" he asked slowly. "Do you really mean that, if I lost everything, you would still marry me?"

A curious expression, an expression almost of fear, flashed into her eyes, but disappeared so quickly that a moment later Dick could not be sure that it had really been there. Then she smiled up at him.

"Of course I mean it, Dick dear," she said; "but for my sake you will try and save something, won't you?"

"If I care to accept an offer which has been made to me, I can avoid altogether coming a cropper," he said.

"But of course you will accept it. You must accept it."

"You say that without knowing what the offer is, and whence it comes. It might be something which I could not honourably accept."

"Tell me what it is, Dick?"

"The man who holds my fate in his hands is staying here at this moment, Dorothy," replied Dick slowly. "It is he to whom I had contracted to make certain deliveries of wheat to-morrow. This morning, however, he came to me and offered to extend the period for a month. If I accept that offer it means I shall avert the crash, for in that time I could get together the wheat asured."

"But you must accept Digby Falkiner's offer, Dick. You must not let any false sense of pride stand in the way. Think, Dick, what it means to me?"

Saunders' hands tightened over hers.

"How did you know it was Digby Falkiner who made that offer to me?" he asked quickly.

Dorothy flushed, then laughed nervously.

"Why—why, Dick, it could only be Digby Falkiner. He is the only man staying here who could possibly be strong enough to break you, and, besides, I know it must have been he, for he, too, is a big market operator."

"You are quite right, Dorothy. It was Digby Falkiner."

"And you will accept his offer, Dick—for my sake?" she pleaded.

He bowed his head.

"If Digby Falkiner's offer is what it appears to be, then I shall accept it, Dorothy," he said slowly.

"Oh, you have made me so happy, Dick," she cried: "and I did so want to be happy to-day. And now I will tell you a secret, Dick dear, but no one else is to know it until to-night. Eleanor Hanington and Digby Falkiner are engaged, and mother is to announce it this evening."

Dick Saunders felt something leap within him. Then he stood, cold and stiff as marble.

"Tell me, Dorothy," he asked quietly, "where did you meet Miss Hanington?"

"Oh, I have known her for years. She is my dearest friend, and I am so happy that she has finally made up her mind to take Digby Falkiner. He has been wanting to marry her for two-years. You know, Dick, we were at school together in Paris."

"It is odd that I have never heard you speak of her before," he remarked.

"Have I never done so? If not, it is because you have always seemed so engrossed in your business, Dick. I want you to know her better, for she is a Canadian, like yourself. Isn't it strange, Dick? I never thought of that before."

"Quite a coincidence," he agreed. "And you say she is to marry Digby Falkiner?"

"Yes. And now, Dick dear, I must run along. You will have to amuse yourself until this afternoon."

She kissed him lightly, then left him. But as she sped across the lawn towards the house, Dick Saunders, gazing after her, was asking himself a question.

"Now, did she know or did she not know of the offer Falkiner had made me before she came to tell me she would marry me whether I came a cropper or not?" he muttered. "Did she really only guess that Digby Falkiner was the man, or did she actually know? I should not have credited Dorothy with so much perception."

And in that moment a tiny seed of doubt was sown in Dick Saunders' mind, which was to grow with startling rapidity. With his eyes on the ground, he did not see a girl coming towards him across the lawn, and only when he heard his name spoken softly did he look up and see Eleanor Hanington standing before him.

It was impossible for Dick Saunders to suppress a startled exclamation.

"Eleanor!" he gasped.

"Yes, Dick," she answered steadily. "It is Eleanor, and I want to talk to you."

Dick bowed his head silently, and, turning, they walked back towards the arbour.

There Eleanor turned and regarded him gravely.

"You have changed a good deal in five years, Dick," she said.

"And you, too, Eleanor," he responded. "We have both come a

long way since those days on the farm, and you, I imagine, have found all that you yearned for."

"I have found the world, if that is what you mean, Dick. And I have also found a little wisdom. I know now that in my very ignorance I was happy, but I did not understand that until I had really found that the glitter which lured me was not all gold. And you, Dick, you, too, have lived during those five years. You went away very suddenly, and—and you did not say goodbye!"

The man was gazing straight ahead of him.

"It would have done no good to say good-bye," he replied dully. "I went away because there was nothing else to do. I found a certain success in the outside world, and three years later I came back for you. But you were gone."

Eleanor gripped his sleeve with her fingers.

"You came back, Dick?" she exclaimed.

He nodded.

"Yes, I came back," he repeated. "The oil discovery had come. You were gone, and no one knew where."

"I never knew you had returned to the valley, Dick," she said softly. "I thought you had forgotten. But I am glad, Dick, and proud that you have achieved. But not until yesterday did I dream that you were the man whom Dorothy was to marry. I, too, am to be married, Dick."

He bowed stiffly.

"I have just been told," he said coldly, "and I congratulate—the man."

Eleanor Hanington had sought Dick Saunders that morning for a particular reason, and she had deemed it essential for her purpose—imperative as a bulwark for herself—to tell him at once of her own engagement to Digby Falkiner. She had come to him with the idea strong in her mind that at any cost Dorothy Brett's happiness must be safeguarded. Her gratitude to the Bretts by no means blinded her to the narrowness of Dorothy's outlook; but to her that was only an added reason why the girl should achieve the little ambitions which filled her. Beyond one occasion when, during the night, she had allowed herself to revel in the exquisite pain of regret, she had loyally put away from her the thoughts which were always with her, and which had surged up with redoubled force since she had seen Dick Saunders again. The strength of character of the girl had mothered a

deep integrity in the woman, and it was with no thought of herself, except in so far as she might become a solving factor in the affair, that she had set herself to straighten out Dorothy's tangle. It seemed to her to be a decree of Fate that she should become this instrument, for it was in her power, as in the power of no one else, to persuade Digby Falkiner to withhold the blow which threatened Dick Saunders' fortune and Dorothy's happiness. She had told herself—she was telling herself now—that it was because of the gratitude she felt towards the Bretts and because of the affection she had for Dorothy, that she had paid the price which she knew Digby Falkiner would expect. She would not permit herself to acknowledge that it was Dick's safety which had been the real inspiration, and even if that suggestion had come to her during the night she had kept it completely away from her since her promise to Digby Falkiner.

She was there to fight for Dorothy's happiness, not her own, and if a price must be paid, it was she who was ready to pay it. Nevertheless, it was impossible for her not to flinch from the stabbing pain of his words. At least Dick would never know, he must never know why she was to marry Digby Falkiner.

"It is not of myself, but of Dorothy, I wish to speak," she hurried on. "Digby—Mr. Falkiner has told me a little of the present situation which exists between you and him. He has also informed me that certain contracts which he thought you might have some difficulty in fulfilling were not essential to him, and that he had offered you a month's extension on them. Dorothy also has told me something of this, Dick, and I want you, for her sake, not to refuse to take advantage of the proposal Digby has made. Dorothy is, by the very force of circumstances, of the conventional type, Dick, and such things mean a lot to her. It would make her happy if you were to do this, and because of—because of our old friendship I have dared to try to persuade you."

"Dorothy is to be congratulated on possessing such a warm advocate," said Dick stiffly. "But I have already told her that I see no reason why I should not accept Mr. Falkiner's offer, which seems sufficient to ensure her happiness and shield her from the gossip which she dreads so."

"I am glad, Dick," responded Eleanor. "It will make me happy, too."

So suddenly did Dick Saunders swing round and grasp her by the shoulders that he startled her.

"It will make you happy, will it?" he said tensely, his eyes burning into hers. "Then I am glad—glad, do you hear? For you it seems an easy matter to find happiness; it was as easy, too, for you to forget the past. Has that last day in the valley faded entirely from your mind? Have you forgotten that it was you, with your cry for freedom, your desire for the outside world, who sent me away? Well, you have had it all now, and you have found your own happiness. Nor is it necessary for you to worry any further about Dorothy's. If money will bring her contentment she shall have it, even though I have to give it to her through—Digby Falkiner."

With that he pushed her from him, and strode abruptly out of the arbour.

As for Eleanor, with hands clutching her breast, she sank to the ground with a low moan of pain. Did she remember that spring day in the valley? Was not every detail of it burnt into her soul?

Then suddenly, as she heard Digby Falkiner's voice in the distance, she sprang to her feet, and, stealing round to the rear of the arbour, sped along a secluded path towards the house, there to endeavour to conquer, once and for all, the agony of remorse which threatened to overwhelm her.

CHAPTER V. Dick Saunders Discovers the Truth.

IT had seemed to Dick Saunders that his mind could have grasped upon no more complicated problem than the one which had faced him the day before. But now, with a reprieve offered him, with Dorothy's happiness practically assured, he found himself in a state of greater mental chaos than before. As he strode through the park he tried desperately to analyse the combination of events which had led up to a solution of his troubles, but at the same time to the state where he was compelled to demand an understanding of his own soul. The doubt he could not help but feel of Dorothy had grown rapidly during the past hour, and now he was able to ask himself judicially if she had known of Falkiner's offer before she came to him. From what Eleanor had said he knew that Dorothy must have talked matters over with her the night before, and certainly Eleanor had known of Falkiner's proposal. Was it not natural, he asked himself, that she should go to Dorothy and console her with the hope that he would accept Falkiner's offer. He knew that Eleanor and Digby Falkiner had gone off together shortly after breakfast, and it was soon after that when Falkiner had come to him. Was it on that occasion he had told Eleanor of the relief he intended offering to Saunders? If so, was it not reasonable to suppose that Eleanor would immediately communicate such an important item of news to Dorothy? At any rate, there would have been just about time for this when Dorothy had come to him, and, to save his life, Dick could not get out of his mind the remembrance of how, during Dorothy's conversation with him, she had revealed the fact that she knew it was Falkiner who held Dick's fate in his hands. He did not want to do her an injustice, but certainly if she had known these things before she came to him, then the protestations she had made were utterly valueless.

He recalled the fleeting look of fear which had appeared in her eyes when he asked her if she would still wait for him should he not accept the way out which offered. And he wondered now what she would say if he were to inform her that he could not see his way clear to reach out for the lifebuoy which Falkiner had thrown him. It was at that point the question of motive obtruded itself. Why had Digby Falkiner done this?

For the last three months he had headed the ring which Dick knew was out to break him. Up to the last moment on Saturday Dick's brokers had failed to get any sort of reasonable quotation of the wheat the ring controlled, and his last information had been that fulfilment of contract would certainly be looked for on Monday. There had been no sign of yielding then on the part of Digby Falkiner or the ring he controlled. Yet on this day, without the slightest warning, and in a most startlingly casual manner, he had informed Dick that the contracts would be extended a month if he desired. Dick knew perfectly well that Digby Falkiner could not grant him this leeway without surrendering the hope of a great portion of the profit which would have been his. Nor was it likely that his colleagues in the ring would look at all kindly on the sudden escape from the trap of the man they had worked so strenuously to break.

There must have been a motive, far stronger than any business consideration, to cause Digby Falkiner to cast away the victory which he had held in his hand. What could that motive have been? Dick remembered now what Dorothy had said about Eleanor's engagement to Falkiner. She had said that Falkiner had been wanting Eleanor to marry him for two years or more, and now, for some reason or other, Eleanor had suddenly yielded.

He wondered if Eleanor was responsible for Falkiner's action. Was it because she wanted Dorothy's happiness so that she had pleaded with Digby Falkiner to do what he had done? If that were so, had she, in turn, given herself as the price of Dorothy's happiness? It never occurred to Dick that his safety might have been the real inspiration; nor could he bring himself to believe that she would marry Digby Falkiner if she did not love him. The solution of it was beyond him; but somehow, he felt that Digby Falkiner's offer was based not upon his own desire to give his opponent a fighting chance, but upon some sort of intriguing on the part of the two girls. It was that which galled Dick Saunders' pride; but, had it not been for Eleanor, he might still have accepted Falkiner's offer.

Fight as he would, however, he could not conquer the throbbing pain which filled him. Since that interview in the arbour, realisation had crashed in upon him ripping asunder the last shreds of the cloud which had dulled remembrance; and now he knew that it was Eleanor, and Eleanor alone, whom he loved, and would always love. And it was that, which made it impossible for him to accept any favours from Digby Falkiner if they came at Eleanor's behest.

It was late afternoon before Dick Saunders got back to the house, and by that time he had determined on two things. He would return to town that night, and in the morning he would go to see Digby Falkiner in an attempt to discover the truth. After making his apologies to Mrs. Brett, and pleading urgent business as an excuse, he sought Dorothy, and told her that he must return to town that night. Their interview was of the briefest, but Dick saw neither Eleanor nor Digby Falkiner again.

He drove straight through to the Albany, where he got on the telephone with his own confidential clerk, and after a hurried dinner he went on to his offices in Mincing Lane. His confidential man was already there, and in his private room Dick Saunders once more went over every detail of the campaign. Together they plodded through all the papers in the matter, from the very first day of its inception, and by the time they had thrashed out each point once more it was past midnight. Then, lighting a cigarette, Dick Saunders pushed the papers from him, and leaned back in his chair.

"Well, Cameron," he said to the other, "what do you think of it?"

"I don't see a single loophole, Mr. Saunders," replied Cameron. "If there had been any solution, we should have found it on Saturday; but it all boils down to this. If we can get hold of the wheat we can swing through. If not, then I see nothing for it, Mr. Saunders, but to default on our contracts."

"I fancy you are right, Mr. Cameron," remarked Dick. "But what would you say if I told you there was a solution?"

"I'd say, sir, that it could only be a miracle," responded Cameron.

"It is just that, Cameron, and the last thing you would ever guess. To-day Digby Falkiner offered to hold over all the contracts for another month."

Cameron stared at his chief in dumbfounded amazement.

"Digby Falkiner offered to do that, sir!" he exclaimed. "Is he mad?"

"I must confess that his action rather puzzles me," rejoined Dick, "and up to now I fail to understand it clearly. Nevertheless, what I have told you is fact. He informed me to that effect to-day."

"Do you think it is a trap of any sort, sir?" asked Cameron.

"Strangely enough, I don't," answered Dick. "I believe Mr. Falkiner is inspired by other-motives."

"That means, then, sir, that we shall be able to get sufficient supplies together from overseas to make deliveries as we have contracted. It means salvation to us, sir."

"If we accept the offer," put in Saunders quietly.

"If we accept! I don't understand you, sir. Surely you will not turn it down, Mr. Saunders. Forgive me for speaking frankly, sir, but if we fail to make delivery or get any extension of time, it means ruin."

"I am perfectly aware of that," responded Dick. "But, at the same time, I have not yet made up my mind whether I shall accept or refuse the offer, nor shall I know until I have seen Digby Falkiner to-morrow morning. I wanted to go through all the figures to-night, though, in order to know to the last fraction exactly where we stood. I will see Falkiner at ten o'clock in the morning, and then come straight on here to let you know what I have decided to do. You might lock up these papers, Cameron. I'll go along now."

And as his employer passed out of the office the faithful Cameron shook his head in puzzled amaze. Dick's attitude was utterly beyond his comprehension.

Dick telephoned from his chambers early the next morning to make an appointment with Falkiner, and at ten o'clock sharp he arrived at Falkiner's offices in Lombard Street. Falkiner had come up early that morning from Surrey, and as Dick walked in he greeted him pleasantly enough.

"Well, Saunders," he said, as Dick sat down. "Have you decided to take advantage of my offer? It still holds good, and if you wish to do so I'll dictate a letter to that effect."

"I don't know—yet," responded Dick slowly. "I want to have a talk with you first."

"Go ahead," said Falkiner easily. "I am listening."

Dick brought his gaze to the level of the other man's eyes.

"Falkiner," he said, "I want to know, and I think I am entitled to know, what inspired you to offer me a month's extension on delivery. The last three months is sufficient proof that you did not do it out of any personal regard for me or my position. It can do no harm now for me to say that for some time past I have known you and your crowd were out to break me. Therefore, I can only assume that you made this offer at the behest of someone else. Up to the close of business on Saturday there was not the slightest sign that you intended extending the date of delivery, and, considering that point, I feel justified in assuming, further, that your offer was inspired by something which

40

occurred at the Bretts' yesterday."

Falkiner smiled faintly.

"Your deductions are not altogether wrong, Saunders," he replied. "I can see no harm in telling you that my offer was inspired by someone else."

"Was it Eleanor Hanington?" demanded Dick swiftly.

"It was Miss Hanington, the lady whom I am going to marry," responded Falkiner. "I might add that her request was, I believe, inspired by her friendship for Miss Brett. I did not know until yesterday that she was so intimate with the Bretts, and, as there is nothing she could ask me that I would not do, therefore, Saunders, I offered you relief."

"Which I refuse to accept," exclaimed Dick, rising. "If that offer had been made in a business way I should have accepted it gladly; but I want no favours from Eleanor—from Miss Hanington."

Digby Falkiner had also come to his feet, and as Eleanor's name slipped from Dick's lips his eyes narrowed.

"You seem to speak of Miss Hanington as one would speak of an old friend," he said coldly. "I was under the impression that you had met her for the first time yesterday. Perhaps, though, I am mistaken."

"Know her!" retorted Dick hotly, "I knew her before you even heard of her! I was born and brought up side by side with her in Canada, although I hadn't seen her for five years until yesterday."

It was something in Dick's tones rather than his words which made Digby Falkiner go white. Well he knew, as he had known for two years, that he did not possess Eleanor Hanington's love; yet he had never considered that another man might hold it, for there was no evidence to reveal it. But now something in Dick Saunders' tones told him that, beyond the gash which that five years had cut in the passage of time, there lay events between Dick Saunders and Eleanor Hanington of which only they two knew.

And in that instant there was born in Digby Falkiner a flaming jealousy of the man before him, a frantic hatred of the past of which he was ignorant. For a long minute the two men faced each other, fighting for control. Then suddenly Digby Falkiner relaxed his tense attitude and sank into his chair.

"The offer I made you, Saunders," he said, in a voice from which he could not entirely suppress emotion, "was made at the request of Miss Hanington, and, I think, inspired by her desire to insure Miss

Brett's happiness. The offer still stands. You can accept it or not, as you wish."

"And I can tell you, here and now," retorted Dick, "that I decline it. I have up till three o'clock to-day to make delivery against sale contracts. If I fail to do so by then, you can post me as a defaulter."

With that he snatched up his hat and started for the door; but before he reached it it swung open, and the next instant Eleanor Hanington stepped into the room. One swift glance told her what must have happened between the two men. Then, bowing curtly, Dick Saunders passed out, leaving her along with Digby Falkiner.

Seething with rage against everything and everyone— a rage born of naught but wounded pride, Dick Saunders strode furiously out of the building, and, hailing a taxi, drove at once to his own offices in Mincing Lane. He went direct to his private room, and, locking the door behind him, sat down at the desk. Putting through a trunk call to the Brett place in Surrey, he sat drumming impatiently on the desk until he was connected. Then, striving desperately to control his voice, he asked for Dorothy. After a short wait he heard her voice on the wire.

"I have called you up, Dorothy," he said, "to tell you that I find it quite impossible for me to accept the offer made to me yesterday by Digby Falkiner. I have just left his office, and have informed him to that effect. I have little hope that to-day will find a solution of my difficulties, and by three o'clock I expect that the thing which I told you I feared will have materialised."

"Are you mad, Dick?" she cried. "I thought we had settled all this yesterday, and that you had agreed to accept it. You seem to think only of yourself."

"I am very sorry, Dorothy, but there are certain elements in this affair which make it out of the question for me to take such a way out. I regret exceedingly for your sake that it must be so, but under no circumstances can I alter my decision. If you do not care to contemplate what I expect is bound to result, then I can only offer you your freedom."

"Which I think I shall be wise to take," she answered sharply. "I had no idea you were this type of man, Richard. I have never been so upset in my life."

"Then you mean that you want to be released," asked Dick.

"To be perfectly frank—yes!"

"Then you may consider your desire gratified," he rejoined curtly, and the next moment hung up the receiver.

Rising from the desk, he raised his arms above his head, as though shaking off the last vestiges of the load which had been weighing him down. Then, outwardly the cool-headed, hard-fighting market operator, he unlocked the door of his private room, and called to Cameron. When the door had closed after the confidential clerk, Dick seated himself at his desk, and said to Cameron:

"I have come to the conclusion that I cannot accept the offer made me by Digby Falkiner. We shall have to try what we can do on purchases during the day. 'Phone all our brokers up at once, and tell them to buy anything that offers. In the meantime, get out some wires and see if you can locate a single cargo due to-day which has not been snapped up by Falkiner's ring. I'll arrange the financial end to take care of purchases. It is our only chance, and a mighty slim one at that, but we'll have a shot at it. Now get busy."

"Everything is ready, sir," responded Cameron. "I made the arrangements, thinking you might refuse Mr. Falkiner's proposal. I'll start things moving at once, sir."

And the next moment Dick Saunders was throwing every ounce of energy into what he thought was to be the fight of his life.

CHAPTER VI. *Digby Falkiner Enters His Gethsemane.*

AS the door closed after Dick Saunders, as he rushed out of Digby Falkiner's office, Falkiner rose, and, while drawing up a chair for Eleanor, succeeded in regaining his composure.

"This is a pleasant surprise," he said quietly. "I did not know you were coming up to town to-day."

"I could not remain down there, Digby. I came up to find out what you were doing about Mr. Saunders."

"Why do you call him Mr. Saunders, and not Dick?" he asked, meeting her eyes fully. "It was 'Dick' and 'Eleanor' between you until five years ago. And why did you not tell me, Eleanor, that you had known him in the past?"

She met his eyes bravely.

"I should have told you, Digby, later on, but I saw no reason for doing so at present. It is true, however, that I knew him in Canada. We grew up side by side."

"And it is because you want to save him, not because you are seeking Dorothy Brett's happiness, that you asked me to extend his contracts," he flamed jealously.

Eleanor came swiftly to her feet.

"You forget yourself, Digby!"

He stood up and faced her.

"I beg your pardon," he said, with his voice once more under control. "I should not have said that, but I have had strong provocation this morning. As for Saunders, he has refused categorically to accept my offer."

Eleanor's face blanched.

"That means that he will be ruined!" she gasped.

"I can see no other outcome," he responded.

"Digby, it must not be! You must save him. I have money myself. I will give you that to use, but you must not let him rush headlong into disaster. He is so young, and he has fought so hard all his life."

If Digby Falkiner had had any doubt about Eleanor Hanington's feelings for Dick Saunders, they vanished at her words. In them was a tender yearning, almost a crooning, which tinges only one thing in all the world— the love of a woman.

Gripping the edge of the desk, Digby Falkiner bent forward, and said huskily:

"Eleanor, answer me one question Do you love Dick Saunders?"

"You have no right to ask me a question like that, Digby," she cried. "You said you were satisfied to possess my future—the past is my own."

"And his," put in Digby bitterly. "But your protest has answered my question."

"Listen, Digby," she pleaded. "Let us put this away from us. Dick Saunders and Dorothy Brett must be happy. I made a compact with you inspired by that desire, and I want to keep it. Won't you please—please, forget the past?"

Digby Falkiner had just opened his lips to reply when the desk telephone rang shrilly. Excusing himself, he lifted the receiver and began to speak. At first Eleanor, whose mind was grappling desperately with the problem which confronted her, paid no attention to his remarks, but after a little something about them caused her to listen, and when he finally hung up the receiver and turned to her, she knew by the expression on his face that it had some bearing on the matter they had just been discussing.

"It was Dorothy Brett," said Falkiner. "Saunders has been on the telephone to her, and has told her that he refused my proposal. He offered to release her, and she has taken it."

"Then Dick —" she began impulsively.

"Then Dick is now free," he finished bitterly. "Dorothy wanted me to find you and to tell you. I did not say you were here."

A pregnant silence followed between them, and, with hands clenched under the desk, Digby Falkiner entered his Gethsemane. Five minutes, ten minutes passed, but something in his stern expression, an almost terrible exaltation which was revealed in his eyes, forbade even Eleanor breaking the silence. Yet she did not guess that in those minutes a man was finding his own soul.

A sharp sigh broke from Falkiner as he suddenly relaxed. Then, without looking at her, he drew a pad and pencil across the desk and began to write. After that he pressed the button on his desk, and, to the clerk who answered the summons, said:

"Put this message through at once, and let me know as soon as the reply comes."

As the clerk took the message and retired, Eleanor Hanington never guessed for a single moment that it was to be telephoned to

Dick Saunders, and that it said: "Request your presence on most urgent matter. Get a taxi and come to my offices at once. Wait in the taxi, but send in word as soon as you have arrived."

For the next ten minutes Digby Falkiner drove himself to talk of everything in the world but that which was uppermost in his mind, and Eleanor Hanington, thinking it was in an attempt to regain his composure, seconded his efforts, not dreaming of the moment for which he was waiting. At the end of ten minutes there was a knock on the door, and a clerk entered.

He nodded silently to Falkiner, who nodded curtly in return. Falkiner rose.

"I have found a solution of the difficulty which confronts us, Eleanor," he said unsteadily. "If you will come with me I will reveal its nature."

Wonderingly, she suffered him to lead her from the office and along the corridor to the street. But not until he had jerked open the door of the taxi which waited at the kerb did she see Dick Saunders sitting in the corner. She started back with a sharp cry, but Digby Falkiner thrust her inside, and slammed the door. In a flash she understood the great renunciation he was making, and all the nobility of her soul protested. Struggling to open the door, she panted:

"Digby, Digby, this must not be! I want to keep my contract. Please—please—"

But, pressing hard against the door, Digby Falkiner said to the driver:

"Go on at once! Don't wait! Drive anywhere!"

"No, no, Digby!" exclaimed Eleanor, still struggling with the door. "It cannot—it must not—"

But then the taxi leaped forward with a jerk, and the next moment she had collapsed, sobbing.

Ten minutes later Digby Falkiner rang for his managing clerk, and when the man had entered he said:

"Roberts, you will at once take measures to release our holdings of wheat. Let the market have all it needs."

"But, sir," protested Roberts, "Saunders' brokers are trying to buy in every direction, and this is the day Saunders was to make delivery, Mr. Falkiner."

"Let Saunders' brokers buy all they desire," replied Digby Falkiner curtly. "That is all, Roberts. See that these orders are carried out without delay. And, Roberts," he added, as the man turned to go, "I do not wish to be disturbed."

As the door closed after the clerk Digby Falkiner arose and turned the key in the lock. Then he went back to his desk, and, seated there, he gazed starkly ahead, seeing what pictures only heaven and himself knew.

THE END.

[17,200 WORDS]

"The Marvel," 1d., every Tuesday.

1.000.711 WOMEN WAR WORKERS.

1st *WOMAN WAR WORKER: How in the world do you manage to keep your hair looking so thick and beautiful? Mine is falling out fast, and, as you see, it has faded terribly.*

2nd *WOMAN WAR WORKER: I found I was losing my hair, but tried "Harlene Hair-Drill," with the splendid result you see. You try it, too, and your hair will grow better than ever. You can get a complete Free Trial Outfit, too.*

How All Can Grow Beautiful Long, Thick and Silky Hair.

SPLENDID 4-IN-ONE TOILET GIFT TO ALL BRITISH WOMEN.

TO-DAY is announced a Splendid Gift to Britain's 1,000,711 Women War Workers—in fact, all British Women who care to write for it. The Gift is that of a 4-in-1 Toilet Set, the use of which will not only check any influences injurious to women's and girls' hair, but will actually enrich its growth in both quantity and quality.

This Gift announced to-day is intended to prove, free of expense, to every woman and girl properly considerate of her hair health and beauty, that neither the munitions or other factory, the office, nor the exposure to the weather or work on the land need injure her hair. It will prove that women's hair will thrive wonderfully in health and beauty when it is cultivated according to "Harlene Hair-Brill."

GROW MAGNIFICENT HAIR.

The growing correspondence to hand daily from Women War Workers proves that all too many are finding that the dust, dirt, and the chemical-charged or close atmosphere of factories *is* injurious to the hair. Others report that the conditions of work on the land coarsen the hair, drying it, and causing it to become brittle, split, break, or fall out.

"This need not be the case," declares the Inventor-Discoverer.

"No parts of the bodily structure," says he, "respond so quickly to proper care as the hair." The vitality of the human hair is extraordinary. Invest only two minutes a day in Harlene "Hair-Drilling" it, and it will surprise everyone to see how magnificently it will improve in both quantity and quality.

The scalp will become free from Scurf, Stickiness, and Clamminess. Each hair will flourish. Each root and shaft will be full-formed, so retaining a strong hold to resist falling out, splitting, and breaking.

COSTS NOTHING TO TRY.

Also your hair will grow with rich colour. It will radiate the fragrance and the halo-like sheen of health and beauty.

And it costs nothing to discover this truth for yourself, thanks to this generous gift of "Harlene Hair-Drill" Toilet Outfits.

This offer, while chiefly made to the women, is *also open to men*, for they need its aid also.

Merely write your name and address on the following Gift Coupon, enclosed with 4d. stamps for return postage, and you will receive by return post:

1. A bottle of "Harlene," the true liquid food for the hair, which stimulates it to new growth. It is Tonic, Food, and Dressing in one.

2. A packet of the marvellous hair and scalp cleansing "Cremex" Shampoo, which prepares the head for "Hair-Drill."

3. A bottle of "Uzon" Brilliantine, which gives a final touch of beauty to the hair, and is especially beneficial to those whose scalp is inclined to be "dry."

4. A copy of the new edition of the "Hair-Drill " Manual giving complete instructions for this two-minute-a-day hair-growing exercise.

After you have tried—*free of cost to yourself*—the extraordinary hair-growing and beautifying influence of the "Harlene Hair-Drill" addition to your daily toilet, you will wish to continue it, and you can obtain from your chemists and stores further supplies as follows: "Harlene" in bottles at 1/1 1/2d., 2/9, and 4/9 (Solidified Harlene in tins at 2/9); "Cremex" Shampoo Powders at 2d. each, or 7 packets for 1/-; "Uzon" Brilliantine, in bottles at 1/- and 2/6. Or post free on receipt of price direct from Edwards' Harlene, Ltd., 20, 22, 24, and 26, Lamb's Conduit Street, London, W.C. 1. Carriage extra on foreign orders. Cheques and P.O.'s should be crossed.

Here is your Gift Coupon. Do not delay.

'HARLENE' GIFT COUPON

To EDWARDS' HARLENE, Ltd.,

20, 22, 24, & 26, Lamb's Conduit Street,

London, W.C. 1.

COSTS NOTHING TO TRY.

Also your hair will grow with rich colour. It will radiate the fragrance and the halo-like sheen of health and beauty.

Dear Sirs,—Please send me your Free "Harlene Hair-Drill" Gift Outfit, as announced. I enclose 4d. in stamps, cost of carriage to any part of the world. (Foreign stamps accepted.)

NAME..

ADDRESS..

Answers Library, 80/6/17.

MONEY!

The Strange Life Story of an Everyday Couple.

By Mabel St. John.

This splendid serial story, which is now at its best, tells how Enid Foster, a laundry girl, met Jim Woods, whose real name is James Curtis Bevanwood. Jim has seen pretty Enid leaving the laundry, and has fallen in love with her.

Jim and Enid are married, and spend their wedding-day at home. Meanwhile, at his fine country seat, Sir Harold Bevanwood lies dying. A lawyer finds out that Jim is heir to the Bevanwood estates, and calls on Enid. Jim comes home excited, when the lawyer tells him that he is Sir James Bevanwood.

Enid and "Sir James," as Jim is now, take up their residence at Bevanwood, where they meet relatives in Sheila Clare and her brother, both of whom are determined, in their crafty way, to drive Jim and Enid apart.

Geoffrey persuades Enid to elope with him. They go away. Sheila is anxious to fill Enid's place, but Jim is very troubled by his young wife's disappearance. He proceeds to carry out a plan that has formed in his mind.

Jim's Plan.

THEN Jim turned away, and the woman stared after him.

"I don't know what made 'im," she said, "nor I don't care; but this I do know—that I wish there was a few more made like him!"

And so the man with the impassive face and the lumbering stride and the aching heart went down the sunny village street, and at the end of the street, where the road turns whiter and rises to the swell of the downs, he met a small, freckled, red-haired boy of about thirteen.

"I been looking for you, Billy Wasser!" he said.

"Well, 'ere I am, governor!" the boy said. "Going to—"

Sir James Bevanwood nodded.

"You come with me, I want to talk with you," he said. "I'm going" —he paused— "going away for a bit."

The boy's face fell.

"Not fur, Billy!" Jim said. "Not so fur as you carn't pop in and see me now and a bit!"

"Oh, you mean there?" the boy said. "Going to live there?"

"That's about the size of it, Billy. You see, it's like this way with me. I've got a bit of thinking to do—a bit of real, 'ard thinking. Things isn't—isn't what they might be, and I've got to think a way out, a best way for—for 'er" —he paused— "best way for everybody; and I don't believe in doin' nothing in a 'urry. I want to think" —he paused— "and when a man's got thinking to do, why 'e carn't be listening to chatter all the time. A man's got to be alone to think properly."

The boy nodded. He looked at his big friend with wise blue eyes.

"So you're going down there to do your thinking?" he said.

"That's it, Billy, that's the idea I got into my 'ead; and you—you're going to 'elp me! You see, I don't want no one to know where I gorn to, otherwise I'd 'ave some of 'em round worrying me. I just want to be alone—all alone! I've got a deal of 'ard thinking to do, Billy, boy!"

"Where do I come in, governor?"

"That's it!" Jim said. "Well, I'll be wanting things. I sha'n't want to come 'ere to get 'em. I sha'n't want no one to know where I am. You got to tell your mother I'm travelling a bit, and I want you to come with me. See?"

The boy's face beamed.

"And—and you mean you'll 'ave me along with you down there?"

"That's it! You'll have to fetch and carry for me. We'll 'ave to git what we want over from Horswood. It's a long tramp; we'll 'ave to git a bicycle."

He paused.

They were on the downs now. He sat down suddenly on the turf, and brought out a pocket-book. From the pocket-book he selected a visiting-card, engraved, "Sir James Bevanwood, Bart., Bevanwood, Amerhurst, Sussex."

"Billy, you got to go back to your mother and tell 'er," he said, "about your coming with me. Say as I met you, and want you; say you'll be away a week or two, maybe a month or two; but you'll be all right with me."

The boy nodded.

"And this'll be so as she'll know it's all right."

Jim nibbled the end of his pencil, and then wrote laboriously:

"To Mrs. Wasser—I want your Billy to come with me. He'll be alright and well looked after, don't worrie about him, so no more at present, from yours truley, James Bevanwood."

He wrote this on the back of the card till it overflowed, so he finished it on the front.

"You take that to 'er, and I'll wait 'ere till you come back," he said.

And then he stretched himself out on the soft turf, and lay staring up at the blue skies; and already James Bevanwood was beginning to think his deep, hard thinking; and the burden of his thoughts was always, "What's the best I can do for 'er?"

The Elopement.

"YOU'LL need things," Geoffrey said. "You can get all you need in London."

"Then we are going to London," the girl said.

"At first. After that we shall leave for the sea. We shall stay at Dover the night and cross by the morning boat to France."

"France! I never been there. It's across the sea," she said.

"You'll enjoy every minute of Paris," he said. "It's a new life for you. I'm opening the book of the world to you, 'Nid, and I shall get my reward in seeing the wonder and delight in your sweet eyes, darling."

"Don't!" she said. "Don't call me that—I don't like it! Some'ow it seems to spoil everything! Just 'Nid'll do!"

He smiled to himself.

They had walked across the downs in the early morning to Horswood; from Horswood they took the train to London. He would need things himself. He must have clothes—just enough to present a creditable appearance. It gave him a thrill of pleasure to see men in the street turn their heads for another glance at the girl beside him. They admired her, and envied him probably. That's what he wanted.

"She belongs to me!" he thought. "Mine entirely. There's no going back now!"

He went with her to do the shopping. He went to the bank and drew out the last penny he had there. He reckoned it would just about see him through, pay for her needs, the trip, and the hotel expenses, and then Sheila was sure to send him a remittance—he could reckon on that!

In order that Sir James Bevanwood should have every possible facility for prosecuting his suit when the time came, he took 'Nid to his own chambers.

His manservant made tea for them. Before Watson, the man, he spoke unguardedly of their future movements.

"We'll stay at Dover to-night; to-morrow we'll cross to Paris," he said. "We'll have a few weeks there. It will be a glorious time; 'Nid, just you and I, together, and alone!"

The man stared, but he said nothing. What should he say?

"Pack me all I shall want for about a month. Don't overdo it, Watson, and if any letters come for me, address them to me at the Hotel Boulogne, Paris."

"Very good, sir," the man said stiffly.

He stared hard at 'Nid.

"Lady Bevanwood and I —"

Geoffrey paused, as though he had let slip something that he had not intended. He saw that the man had heard, and he smiled to himself.

An hour later they were in the train for Dover, and she, tired out, wondering a little, frightened a little, ill at ease, fell asleep. She slept as soundly and as sweetly as a child might, rocked and lulled by the movement of the train. And, watching her, a great consuming passion for her came to him.

He watched the dark shadows of her lashes against her cheeks, the red rose mouth of her, the wonderful hair, the unstudied grace of her attitude, the little, childlike hands. He bent forward. He fell on his knees and pressed his lips to her hands, softly as not to waken her.

He knew it was the passion, the love of his life, the love compared with which all other loves had been savourless, commonplace, and ordinary. He even made himself believe that all the rubbish of love in a previous stage of existence had really been between him and her. He wanted to believe it.

When she woke she found his burning eyes on her, and she shivered with a new fear, a new dread. But she was tired, the sleep had made her dull and heavy. She wanted only to rest, to go to bed and rest and sleep till the morning came.

They went to an hotel.

"Will you stop at the same hotel as me?" she asked.

"Will I —why, of course!" he said. "Don't you wish it, 'Nid?"

"I don't know as I thought—that I thought about it," she said wearily. "All I wants is to go to sleep. I'm tired—tired to death! I don't know—"

She paused. She thought of Jim; she fancied she could see the pain and surprise in his face. She did not want to hurt him; he had been very good to her— very good, except twice! Remembering that twice, she shivered a little.

He had ordered a private sitting-room, where the dinner was served. 'Nid had no appetite. She was haunted by this vision of Jim— Jim suffering, Jim with pained eyes. Yes, he had been good to her in many, many ways. He had not sent her back to work at the laundry, for one thing, as some men did. He had made life pleasant for her. It was Jim who had first taken her to see the sea.

"Darling, what are you thinking of?" he said.

He had been studying her face eagerly, his own eyes glowing.

She started.

"I arst you not to —to call me that!" she said, with quiet dignity. " Some'ow it don't sound right! I'm thinking I'm tired. I want to go to bed and to sleep. My head aches, and I'm a bit worried. It'll be all right in the morning. Can I go now?"

"Yes, why not? Go now!" he said.

He rose.

"Oh, 'Nid!" he cried suddenly. "Just you and I alone—you and I! The thing I have hoped for, prayed for, longed for, darling! My beloved!"

His pent-up passion found expression at last. He caught her in his arms, he held her, struggling, he kissed her, not once, but many times. He smothered her face in kisses. He kissed her hair, her dainty little ears, her nose, her eyes, her lips, and over her there came the sickly feeling of helpless disgust, of growing horror, of actual fear.

She broke from him at last, broke away by main force.

"I—I'm going to bed!" she said, "to sleep. I—I'm ill, tired."

She hardly knew what she was saying. She only knew that suddenly she hated him, that her very soul was filled with disgust of him, and a great fear, a bodily fear, a horror that banished weariness and sleep, came to her. He had shown her to the door of the room that was to be hers.

"So good-night, my beloved!" he said. "Good-night!"

His eyes burned into hers.

And then he was gone, and she had locked the door; but she paced the room restlessly like a caged thing. Then suddenly she made up her mind.

She turned the key in the lock, and opened the door cautiously. She peeped out. It was late now, and the hotel was all quiet. She had put on her hat and her cloak. She had taken her few possessions, leaving the things that he had bought for her. And now she crept down the stairs till she gained the hall. A night porter stared at her.

"I'm going—going out," she said unsteadily. "My head is bad; it aches badly. I want to walk. The night air'll do me good. I shall be back soon."

He opened the door to her, and she went out. She found herself in unfamiliar streets under the cool night sky. Once she looked back, only once, and then she walked on and on, far into the night, till she had left the town behind her. She walked on through deserted, silent country roads, through little sleeping hamlets, walked till the dawn was in the sky and the rose tint of the new day made the world beautiful.

Jim and the Boy.

"A BOY brought it —Mrs. Wasser's boy. He said there was no answer, and he has gone."

Sheila Clare nodded. She took the note. It bore her own name scrawled in the unformed, schoolboy hand of Jim Bevanwood.

"What message has the idiot sent me?" she wondered, as she tore the envelope open.

As she read her brow puckered in a frown. There was a lack of understanding in her eyes.

"What does it mean? What has he gone for, and where to? Not— not to seek for her? Good heavens, he couldn't be such a fool as that!"

"Dear Sheela," the letter ran,— "I'm going away for a bit. I want to be alone, to do a bit of thinking. Don't worrie about me. I'm all right. Look after yourself, and have all you want like the place was your own. You're mistress, anyway, till I come back. I've got to think out the best for everyone, including what you said to me to-day; also 'Nid and him, too.—Yours truley,

"J. BEVANWOOD."

"Fool!" the woman said.

She went to the window and stared out into the grounds. Where had he gone? On what wild, senseless chase? Surely not—not to

Paris, to look for 'Nid and Geoffrey? She stamped her foot with sudden rage. The man was enough to drive her mad. However, he was gone, and, as he had said, she was mistress here till he came back, at any rate—and then probably afterwards. But it would have been more satisfactory to have him here under her influence.

She did not like this breaking away—did not like it at all.

"But he will come back soon. The fool will feel lost without me to advise him," she thought.

Jim Bevanwood took quiet possession. It was his own property. He sent Billy Wasser over to Horswood. It was seven miles, but he knew that the boy could trudge it in a little over two hours. He had implicit faith in Billy's honesty. He provided Billy with more money than the youth had ever seen in his life.

"You get a bike, and come back on it for one thing," Jim said. "Then you got to 'ave a few things here, Billy, to be comfortable. Git all them things I've writ down—soap and tea and sugar and bread. Then you take this 'ere bit of paper to Saunders, the furnishing shop. We'll make it real comfortable 'ere."

He had thought of everything, or as nearly everything as a man can think of when it comes to housekeeping. During the coming days he would realise that for everything he had thought of he had forgotten two other necessary articles. But these were merely details.

Jimmy was gone with the money and the written instructions, and Jim Bevanwood set to work. He found a battered old pail, which he filled at the stream before the front door. He swamped the floor of the sitting-room; then with his large pocket-knife he set to work to trim the creepers and ivy into something like order over the windows and door of his new home. It kept him occupied. The time flew by surprisingly quickly. Presently he heard a cart coming down the white chalk road, and he stepped across the stream to the broken down gate to see what it was. It was Saunders' cart from Horswood, bringing him the things he had ordered. The man driving it was a stranger to him, he to the man. Jim Bevanwood, in his shirt-sleeves, his face well blackened from the dust in the ivy, and looking generally disreputable, did not suggest Sir James Bevanwood, of Bevanwood, to the man.

"Hello, mate!" he said. "Is this the shanty this stuff is for?"

"I expect so," Jim said. "Bring it in. I'll lend a 'and!"

They carried the contents of the cart into the shanty. Two small iron bedsteads, with their complement of sheets and blankets, a roll of linoleum, a couple of brooms, two cane-seated chairs, a dozen and one other articles, including a kettle and a good, useful, all-round saucepan.

"Phew!" the man said. "You ain't living in this 'ole, are you, mate?"

"Going to," Jim said, "for a bit. Out of the world, ain't it?"

"Forgotten 'ole, I call it!" the man said. "Some people know their own business best!" he added thoughtfully.

He looked at Jim. He wondered if this man was a criminal hiding from the law which he had outraged. There was nothing very criminal in Jim Bevanwood's appearance.

" 'Armless lunatic, I expect," the man thought, as he drove away.

The arrival of the goods gave Jim something more to do. He set to work with the broom. He put up one small iron bedstead in one top room, the other in the other. He made the beds as cleverly as a woman might. Sir James Bevanwood, to the manner born, might not have understood the making of a bed. Jim Woods had made his own many a score of times. He had done it for himself; there was nothing strange to him in all this.

Considering its natural drawbacks, he had got the place very ship-shape when Billy Wasser came back, riding his new bicycle, and with a sack of provisions slung over his stout little shoulders.

"'Ow's it beginning to look, Billy?" Jim said.

"Fine!" the boy said. "You been workin' all right, ain't you? Got the beds up and all! What do you think of the bike?"

"Ripping!" Jim said. "'Ow much?"

"Five-ten. 'E wanted five and a 'arf guineas. I beat 'im down the five-and-six, and he wouldn't, gi' a bell in, neither, so I sneaked one!"

"You take that there bell back next time you go to Horswood," he said. "Sneakin' ain't the game, Jimmy!"

"But after paying 'im for the bike —" the boy complained.

"You ain't no right to sneak the bell," Jim said. "It ain't right, Billy. It's wrong. You take it back!"

Billy looked at his master resentfully, then his face cleared. No one, no child, could look resentfully at Jim Bevanwood for long.

"All right, governor. I'll ride over and take it back to-morrow, and tell 'im I made a mistake, the dirty 'ound!"

58

For the first time for many months a fire was lighted in the little rusty old kitchen grate. Billy Wasser brought in the wood, of which there was no lack, Jim lighted it. He boiled water and made tea, which they drank without milk, for the best of all reasons. He fried some bacon and some eggs, which he broke into the pan in masterly fashion.

They sat opposite one another at a small deal table, and beamed at one another.

"This is something like!" Billy Wasser said. "You ain't 'arf a cook, you ain't, governor!"

"I can do a bit that way," Jim said modestly.

(Another fine instalment next week.)

This Week's Economy Hint
Mixed dried fruit and BIRD'S Custard *Hot*.

At all grocers, a mixture of dried apricots, prunes, apples, etc., is now on sale. It is inexpensive, and requires very little or no sugar.

DIRECTIONS: — Soak, rinse and stew the fruit till tender.

Make the Bird's Custard in the usual way, and pour over the fruit Hot, or serve a little of both on each plate.

The fruit is naturally wholesome; Bird's Custard adds the all-important nutriment. Together they make a dish that is always very delicious, very satisfying, and a real money saver.

BIRD'S — the *Nutritious* Custard is sold in Pkts, boxes and large Tins.

Printed and published weekly by the Proprietors, at The Fleetway House, Farringdon Street, London, Engand. Subscription, 7s. per annum,

For Advertising Spaces, address Advertisement Manager. Other communications to 'Answers Library' Offices, The Fleetway House, Farringdon Street, London, E.C. 4.

Agents for the Colonies: GORDON & GOTCH, London; Melbourne; Sydney; Brisbane; Perth. W.A. Wellington, N.Z.; Christchurch, N.Z. A.L.

Agents for South Africa; Central News Agency, Limited.

The "AMBROSE WILSON" MAGNETO CORSET

Mr. Ambrose Wilson's Marvellous Invention is now within the reach of every woman who fills in and sends the Coupon below.

FROM the moment when you put them on a ceaseless stream of Magnetic Power permeates your whole body from head to heel. The joy of New Life, of New Health and New vigour thrills through every nerve. You feel a different woman. Your outlook upon life is different— brighter, happier, and more hopeful.

Think for yourself what it means to be thoroughly healthy, always to enjoy life, not for an hour, not for a day, but for always. I want you to send for a pair of my Magneto Corsets, and join the vast and increasing army of happy wearers of this most wonderful invention.

The price of my Corset is not pounds, it is only shillings. The price is 6s. 11d., but I do not ask you to send that amount. All I ask is that you send me a postal order for 1s., and I will send you a pair of my Magneto Corsets that will fit you like a glove. It will be a red-letter day to you the day you receive the Corsets, because it will be the beginning of new life.

They are modelled on the most up-to-date lines, perfect fitting, graceful, and charming—but they are MORE. They are Life-giving, because they contain Nature's great revitaliser — Magnetism. From the moment when you put them on you are surrounded by Magnetic Force, which your body absorbs naturally and freely. There are no shocks, no batteries. The Magnetic current passes right through the body from head to heel, revitalising every nerve, every muscle. New Health and New Life come to you.

(See Coupon below.)

Beauty, Charm, Grace, and, above all, GOOD HEALTH assured to all who wear the Ambrose Wilson Magneto Corset.

The "AMBROSE WILSON"
MAGNETO CORSET
SENT FOR **1/-**
(See Coupon below.)

Mr. Ambrose Wilson's Marvellous Invention is now within the reach of every woman who fills in and sends the Coupon below.

Beauty, Charm, Grace, and, above all, GOOD HEALTH assured to all who wear the Ambrose Wilson Magneto Corset.

FROM the moment when you put them on a ceaseless stream of Magnetic Power permeates your whole body from head to heel. The joy of New Life, of New Health and New vigour thrills through every nerve. You feel a different woman. Your outlook upon life is different—brighter, happier, and more hopeful.

Think for yourself what it means to be thoroughly healthy, always to enjoy life, not for an hour, not for a day, but for always. I want you to send for a pair of my Magneto Corsets, and join the vast and increasing army of happy wearers of this most wonderful invention.

The price of my Corset is not pounds, it is only shillings. The price is 6s. 11d., but I do not ask you to send that amount. All I ask is that you send me a postal order for 1s., and I will send you a pair of my Magneto Corsets that will fit you like a glove. It will be a red-letter day to you the day you receive the Corsets, because it will be the beginning of new life.

They are modelled on the most up-to-date lines, perfect fitting, graceful, and charming—but they are MORE. They are Life-giving, because they contain Nature's great revitaliser — Magnetism. From the moment when you put them on you are surrounded by Magnetic Force, which your body absorbs naturally and freely. There are no shocks, no batteries. The Magnetic current passes right through the body from head to heel, revitalising every nerve, every muscle. New Health and New Life come to you.

"ON APPROVAL." COUPON. POST TO-DAY.

To Mr. AMBROSE WILSON, 242, Allen House, 70, Vauxhall Bridge Road, London, S.W. 1.

Simply write your FULL name and address on a piece of paper, fill in your correct measurements, pin Coupon to paper, and post it to me at once.

Please send me a "Magneto Corset" on approval, also full Printed Particulars. I enclose 1s., and if I do not immediately return Corset, I will pay you the balance of 5s. 11d., either in one sum or by weekly instalments of 1s.

IMPORTANT.—Cross the P.O. thus // and make it payable to Ambrose Wilson, Ltd., at G.P.O., London.

Size of Waist.................... Bust.................... Hips....................

NOTE.—*Foreign and Colonial Orders must be accompanied by the full amount and 1s. 6d. extra to pay postage.*

IN PLACE OF POTATOES.

Until potatoes are available, make fritters and rissoles with rice, flaked maize, oatmeal, lentils, etc., fried in "ATORA" Block Suet. The result is very delicious and nourishing. The piquant flavour of an added pinch of Hugon's Sauce Powder makes a real treat. Your Grocer sells "ATORA," Shredded for Puddings, etc., and in solid Blocks for frying, in 1 lb. and ½ lb. boxes.

(ADVT.)

ANOTHER BIG PRIZE LIST!

First Prize £200 **NEW SIMPLETS** First Prize £200

Second Prize, £20; 5 Prizes of £2 10s. each; 50 Prizes of 5s. each; 500 Prizes of 2s. 6d. each.

1,000 PRESENTATION COUPONS, each of which entitles the winner to four FREE efforts in a subsequent competition.

Competitors who require further entrance-forms should purchase *Answers* Every Tuesday, 1d.

THE WAY TO MAKE NEW SIMPLETS.

In order to win one of the above magnificent prizes you should take one of the examples given in the next column or choose ANY ONE word, or TWO, THREE, or FOUR consecutive words in this issue, or the current number of "ANSWERS." Then think out a phrase of not more than four words which has some relation to the example or words chosen. One of the words of the phrase must have at least one letter which is also contained in the example. The other words may contain any letters, whether they are in the example or not.

FOR INSTANCE :
EXAMPLE : Apalling momenT.
NEW SIMPLET : Trying To sack cook.
EXAMPLE : A scrap of paper.
NEW SIMPLET : Created a Record Spill.

EXAMPLES.

In the air	When George was gazetted
The submarine commander said	My lucky number
When profiteers confer	Astonishing luck
Writing on the wall	Dreadful rumour
The postman's knock	We like to think
Forty-one to fifty	Plenty of potatoes
After the fight	Then he woke up
No hurry	In her spare time
A broken reed	The chickens next door
German airmen	My youngest said
She did not like	In the newspapers
Wilful waste	Why not try again ?
Getting shorter	A Blighty one
My Sunday newspaper	Quite enough
Mother's great day	War bread

P.O. No..........
Closing Date, Wednesday, July 11th.   No. 62.

I enter *Answers* No. 62 New Simplets Competition In accordance with the rules and conditions given in *Answers*, and agree to accept the published decision as final and legally binding.

SIGNED ....

ADDRESS ....

EXAMPLE : Page......Column......Line......   ....
Or from above list.

NEW SIMPLET..
(Not more than four words may be used. Send the whole coupon even if only one example is used.)

EXAMPLE : Page......Column......Line......   ....

NEW SIMPLET..
(A Sixpenny postal-order must accompany this coupon. Stamps not accepted.)

If both coupons are sent each must be signed.

P.O. No..........
Closing Date, Wednesday, July 11th.   No. 62.

I enter *Answers* No. 62 New Simplets Competition In accordance with the rules and conditions given in *Answers*, and agree to accept the published decision as final and legally binding.

SIGNED ....

ADDRESS ....

EXAMPLE : Page......Column......Line......   ....
Or from above list.

NEW SIMPLET..
(Not more than four words may be used. Send the whole coupon even if only one example is used.)

EXAMPLE : Page......Column......Line......   ....

NEW SIMPLET..
(A Sixpenny postal-order must accompany this coupon. Stamps not accepted.)

Envelopes must be addressed *Answers'* New Simplets, No. 62, Box 651, The Fleetway House, Farringdon Street, London, E.C. 4.

NOTE.—The Rules governing the Competition will be found in "Answers."

Next week's splendid novel : "Her Strange Employer." By Sidney Drew.